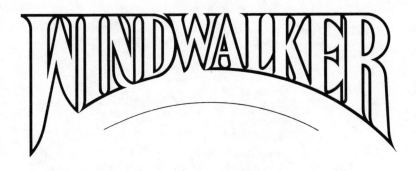

WINDWALKER

Blaine M. Yorgason
Brenton G. Yorgason

Illustrations by Blaine M. Yorgason

Second Edition
Revised and Enlarged
Based on the story from the movie

Bookcraft
Salt Lake City, Utah

Library of Congress Catalog Card Number: 80-70130
ISBN 0-88494-415-8

Second Edition
First Printing, 1980

Lithographed in the United States of America
PUBLISHERS PRESS
Salt Lake City, Utah

To those with the courage
to seek until they find

Contents

Introduction

As Indians, we are moved when we contemplate the Wind-walker, an old man who is a child of Mother Earth and the Great Creator. Through him we see the spirit of our people, a people with total reverence for life — reverence for Earth-maker, the Giver-of-life; for our relationship with Him; for the earth, which is seen not as an object for exploitation but as an insepa-rable part of existence and a complement in forming eternity.

Our people believe that Giver-of-life created the Mother Earth, water, plants, mountains, rocks, man, and all elements in this world. By respectfully acknowledging that each creation has a spirit and an intellect and thus is brother to all others, we express respect and reverence to Giver-of-life. Thus seeking har-mony, we find peace. In *Windwalker* this belief is brought out magnificently. The book is written with a reverent approach which is apparent even in the battle between the old man and the grizzly, where the reader feels the true meaning of this har-mony and peace.

Similarly reverent is the approach as the old man talks with Giver-of-life. He presents himself in the third person, as a friend making an introduction to another. In truth the friend is him-self. For our people this method conveys respect. This is how they offer themselves in prayer. A first-person approach to Deity would not be reverent.

Although *Windwalker* personifies the philosophy of life of the Plains Indians in the story of an old man, it is more than that. It is a story of profound love. In addition, it is a story of age, its wisdom and its memories, a story of teaching, humor, suffering, triumph, and peace. Thus it is essentially a story about each of us. In writing it, the authors have evidenced a remarkable ability to see life outside their own culture and portray that culture with profound dignity and insight, in simple but powerful expression.

John C. Rainer, Jr.
Taos Pueblo — Creek — Cheyenne

Verenda Dosela Rainer
San Carlos Apache

Part One

The Sweat-Lodge

A gust of icy wind rattled new snow against the door-flap of the earthen lodge, wrapping freezing fingers around the edges of the hide, lifting, tugging, groping mercilessly into the darkened lodge.

Grimacing with new pain the old man struggled to pull the buffalo robe more tightly around his shoulders, wishing as he did so that the fire before him was a little larger.

The sounds of the winter camp being disbanded drifted faintly to his ears, and the old man shook his head in deep despair. He had seen it happen before, had even counseled others to do as his family was now doing. But then it was different. Then it was not *him* who was causing the agony.

The way of the Cheyenne was a hard way, the old man knew, but it was also the true way. It was the way of the ancients. A winter camp was never moved. Never, that is, except for sickness. And now the sickness had come to his people. They were leaving, he was too old and too weak to move, and so his family must remain with him until his departure into the land of the Sky People. And that was what was wrong! It was not a good thing that his family perish because the Great One had not yet chosen to take him in death. And perish they would, either from hunger or from roving enemies, for alone his family was not strong enough to provide for or defend themselves.

Oh, Grandfather, the old man moaned,
Why is it that this ancient warrior should . . .

Suddenly the door-flap was pulled aside, and Smiling Wolf, the old man's son, stooped and entered the lodge. With manly dignity he remained for a moment in silence, and then quietly he seated himself across the fire from the withered frame of his father.

Though the old man's eyes were dimmed with age, a father's pride enabled him to see vividly his warrior son. Powerfully built, the man was larger in stature than his father had ever been. There was about him an easy confidence, a grace that reminded his father of nothing so much as Tashina, she who had been mother to this great warrior. Yet behind the old man's pride remained the pain, the agony of knowing that because of his lingering, his only living son had lost his position of leadership among The People. In addition, the young warrior might very well suffer death, himself, before the season of cold would pass.

Following an appropriate silence which denoted respect for his aging and ailing father, Smiling Wolf quietly spoke.

My Father, The People had no meat to leave in our lodge. It has been a time of hunger for us all. Your son must leave you now that he might find food for his family.

The old man dropped his head, blinking rapidly to turn back the tears that were swimming before his eyes.

Smiling Wolf, rising to his feet, noticed, and gently reached out, placing his hands upon the shoulders of his father.

What is this, my father, tears of pain?

Sheetshe, no.
The tears spring from gratitude
that the great Wanken tanka has given

this old warrior
such a fine son.

Feebly then, the old man grasped the arms of his son, doing his best to smile. But then the door-flap was pulled aside once more, a draft of cold air rushed in, and the old man fell back against his robe-covered backrest.

Smiling Wolf turned to see his two small sons, Spotted Deer and Horse-that-follows, gazing fearfully into the dimly lit lodge. Gesturing for them to enter with the thin broth that was their grandfather's meal, the warrior looked once more at his father, nodded approvingly at his sons, and stepped quickly from the lodge.

Staggering against the icy blasts of wind, Smiling Wolf moved across the now-abandoned camp to where his two wives, Dancing Moon and Little Feather, and his tiny daughter, Happy Wind, stood holding his war-horse. As he approached, the horse stomped its hoof impatiently, and Little Feather, her voice full of fear and anger, spoke.

Has not the old fool yet taken his journey to the west?

Be silent, my sister, Dancing Moon whispered apprehensively. *Do you not remember that the old one is the father of our husband?*

That may be true, but because he does not die we have all been left behind by our people. If we do not die from the sickness that dwells in this place, then we will surely perish, if not by cold or by hunger, then by our enemy, the Crow.

Smiling Wolf, hearing their conversation, chose wisely to ignore it. Silently and swiftly he mounted, and turning his horse, he looked down at his two wives.

This warrior goes after food that your bellies will no longer complain.

He then looked directly at Little Feather. *Perhaps when your belly is full your tongue will stop complaining also.*

Subdued, the two women watched in silence as their husband disappeared into the blinding whiteness of the storm-shrouded timber. And as they watched they were completely unaware that they, too, were being observed by the old man.

Oh, Great One, the old warrior wailed, seemingly oblivious to the two boys who were still trying to feed him.

How is it that this old creature
yet lives,
while all around him
have gone to the land
of the Sky People?
This man is but a burden
and such burdens
ought not to be.

Suddenly the old man sank back onto the buffalo robe, a fierce pain gnawing within his withered old body. Apprehensively the two boys watched as their grandfather's chest heaved and his breathing slowed to ragged gasps. But then, just as Spotted Deer was about to call for his mother, the old man's agony passed, his breathing became regular, and all that remained to indicate his torture were the beads of sweat upon his wrinkled brow.

After a long moment of silence, little Horse-that-follows, who at six summers had lived two seasons less than his older brother, but who was nearly as large and equally as inquisitive, suddenly asked the old man a question.

Grandfather, he asked innocently, *why is it that you have not died?*

Startled, the old man pulled himself upright so that he could see more clearly these two boys who were seed of his seed and therefore so much a part of him. Yes, the sincerity was there in both of their faces, as he knew it would be. Like their father these boys would one day be fine men. They deserved an answer. Yet how could he answer when he, himself, did not know, did not understand the thinking of the great Wanken tanka, the great Grandfather.

Perhaps, he said,
his old eyes twinkling,
this old man has not
died
because he would miss

the smiles
of your mothers.

The boys, aware of the constant complaining of Little Feather especially, and even occasionally of their mother, Dancing Moon, giggled and then turned their faces to hide their smiles.

The old man, enjoying their laughter, waited until they were through before he continued.

My young sons,
this man does not know
how to answer
your question,
for he too
has recently wondered
of it.
He knows he is what others
call old,
and old things die. Always.
Yet your grandfather
was not always old
and only recently has
begun
to think of himself
as such.

The boys stared, wide-eyed, and again it was Horse-that-follows who spoke.

Do you mean that you were once a boy? Like us?

My son,
old men do not
grow
from young girls.
As this man was once young,
like you,
so one day you will be
old
like your grandfather.

For a moment the boys thought of what the old man had said, but it was more than they could understand, and so the thought was quickly pushed aside — all except the fact that once the old man had been young. In that thought young Spotted Deer sensed a story, and so eagerly he pursued it. With an air of self-assurance and great wisdom he turned to his younger brother and spoke.

Of course our grandfather was young. He was once a great warrior, like our father.

But Grandfather, he said, speaking now to the old man, *what was it like when you were a boy, like us? Were you a mighty warrior even then?*

Ah, my little ones, the old man sighed as he sank slowly back against his willow backrest, obviously thinking of their question. And as his memory worked he failed to notice, for the first time in many days, the frigid wind which blasted against the mud and willow frame of the sweat-lodge, and which again groped around the edges of the elk hide door-flap, seeking to entwine the old man in its icy grip. For the moment he was lost in the misty realities of his memories, and as his mind drifted back a gentle smile enlivened the wrinkled fatigue of his ancient face.

Part Two

The Lost Son

My sons, the old man began softly,
a man does not,
one day,
become a man.
Instead, when he is very young
he desires greatly to be
a man,
and does his best to do
man things
even then.
Thus, as the seasons of his
life flow by,
each day brings him closer
to true manhood
in one thing
or another.
True manhood comes
over many seasons,

one effort and one experience
at a time.
   Now, when this man was
very young,
perhaps five summers . . .

And so the old man began to unfold before his two grandsons
the story of his life. It was a lengthy telling, even in ways a
tangled one, and yet much there was which remained unsaid.
Still, through it all, the old man found woven, to his surprise, a
thread, a single thread of purpose, of love. And the name of
that thread of memory, she to whom he had given his all, was
Tashina.

   There was a day, the old man continued,
when the warm wind
danced
through the aspen leaves,
along the streams,
and the sunlight
played
with shadows
across the wide
land.
   On that morning this man,
who thought himself a warrior
even then,
took his new bow
and began a hunt,
thinking only of the glory his first kill
would bring.
   As he left his lodge
to begin his stalk
through the brush
of the valley floor,
he found himself followed
by one who,
up to that day,
had been a great

nuisance
in his life.
Her name was Tashina,
she who would one day
become
the mother of your father.

With growing excitement that brought a happy gleam to the old man's weakened eyes, he told of how he and little Tashina had wandered until they had come suddenly upon a small herd of grazing buffalo. With a great show of authority he had placed Tashina behind him, cautioning her to absolute silence. And then, directing her to follow at a safe distance, he worked his way along a ravine to within a few yards of a large young bull.

His heart pounding, the five-year-old boy had pulled his tiny arrow clear to the point. Taking careful aim, he let go, and together he and Tashina watched the shaft arch through the air, slam against the head of the bull, and hang there for an instant. The buffalo bull, puzzled by the slight disturbance, turned, and as it did so the arrow, which had not even begun to penetrate the thick hide, fell ineffectually to the ground.

This warrior, the old man continued,
felt great humiliation,
not because he had not killed,
but because a woman
had seen his
failure.
But Tashina,
my sons,
understood,
for she took a feather from
her hair,
and with great dignity
made
a gift,
the first of many such,
thereby showing her respect for
the courage

of this man who was then
a boy.

The old man leaned once more against his backrest, smiling contentedly as his mind danced across the memories of those long ago, almost forgotten years. The boys, building up the fire, pleaded with their grandfather to tell them more, for surely he had been brave when he was young, and there was much yet to tell.

My sons, the old man said, smiling gently,
when a man is young
it is not always
easy
to tell the difference
between being
brave —
and being foolish.
This man,
when he was young,
did a few brave things as well as many
foolish things.
*   Yet this*
is not the day
for those tellings.
This day an old heart
aches a little
with loneliness,
and an old spirit
sours
with memories.
My sons,
this man will tell you
of how he came to purchase
Tashina.
*   In the encampment of*
The People
there was one, a man
filled

with much jealousy and
much hatred. He was called
Crooked Leg.
   He was old. He had
a wife already,
and much wealth.
Yet more than all else
he desired
Tashina,
the woman of
this man's
heart.

And so the old man talked on, telling of the day he had finally found the courage to take his two horses and offer them for Tashina. Yet Crooked Leg had chosen that day also, and was already at the lodge of Tashina's grandfather offering many horses and many fine robes.

When the young man approached, Crooked Leg turned and, laughing, made a mock of him and his offering. Humiliated, the young man fled from the camp, where with two of his friends he set out on a raid to find other horses. Ultimately, more than successful, the three found a Crow camp and took from them their entire herd, over a hundred head.

Returning with a great show of triumph, the three young men drove the entire herd into the village just as Crooked Leg was making his final offer, an offer of five horses. Instantly, all was pandemonium as the young warrior's horses filled the camp and milled about in total confusion. Crooked Leg's horses, caught up in the melee, roughly jerked their owner from his feet and dragged him away from Tashina and her grandparents. The young warrior then rode up, and with much dignity offered the entire herd for the hand of Tashina. The grandfather very happily agreed, and after the prescribed manner of The People, the young man and Tashina had become one.

As the boys listened intently, the old man talked on, telling of his love for the young maiden and of the joy they found in each other. At length the young woman was heavy with child, and the old man told of his surprise when, upon entering the lodge

one day, he found she had given him twins, two fine sons who
would grow to bless his life.

Grandfather, Spotted Deer interrupted, *was our father one of
these sons?*

The old man nodded, and Spotted Deer continued.

Then where is our father's brother?

For a long moment the old man was silent, struggling with the
pain of his memories. But then, closing his eyes against the tears
which filled them, he continued in his quiet way to answer the
boy's questions.

My little ones, the old man said softly,
it is good that
the joy of remembering is
as strong as the
pain,
for that cuts like
a knife.
Yet, for you, this old man
will answer.

And so he spoke then of two hoops of happiness, when Old
Man Winter did not settle in so hard during the times of hunger,
and when the berries broke the bushes with their weight during
the seasons of plenty. In the young warrior's lodge there was
much in the way of joy, and much togetherness with his woman
and his growing twin sons.

But Crooked Leg was not a happy man, and so with his
woman he left the sacred hoop of The People to begin a wandering. Even that, however, did not drive the thought of Tashina
from his mind, and as one season passed to another his bitterness grew. At length his own woman broke a stick before him
and returned to her people, and Crooked Leg, very lonely,
reacted by joining a renegade Crow encampment. Still his
thoughts were of Tashina, and so at last the day came when he
persuaded a few of the Crow, including a strange and cruel
young man with a badly disfigured eye, to make a raid against
the lodge where Tashina had found happiness with the young
warrior and her twin sons.

The raid came on a day when the young warrior and Tashina
were teaching their sons to swim.

It was a good day,
my sons,
when all the world was
laughing
with this man and
his family.
Smiling Wolf had not yet
dared to swim,
but his brother,
Grey Hawk,
Wohkpiaino,
was nearly to his mother when
Crooked Leg
and the Crow
broke from the trees
to take Tashina.

In the agony of his memory the old man's voice dropped and
the boys strained to hear his description of the brief yet bloody
battle.

As Crooked Leg and the Crow warriors attacked, Tashina
instinctively grabbed up Grey Hawk and fled toward the trees.
The young warrior, instantly aware of what was happening,
took Smiling Wolf and swam swiftly for shore, where he was at
once surrounded by three Crow warriors on horseback. Taunt-
ingly they struck at him with their coup-sticks, imprisoning him
in waist-deep water between their horses.

Fighting desperately to protect his son Smiling Wolf, the
young warrior watched helplessly as Crooked Leg snatched up
Tashina and dragged her struggling body onto his mount.

Crazy with anger, the young warrior attacked the three
Crows, slaying one with the Crows' own coup-stick and nearly
drowning another as he struggled desperately to reach his captured wife. She, meanwhile, had fought so wildly against
Crooked Leg that his horse had reared in fright, throwing them
both to the ground. Instantly, Tashina was on her feet and run-

ning, trying to reach the trees where Grey Hawk had success-
fully hidden. But the young Crow warrior, the cruel one with
the misshapen eye, bore down upon her with his horse. Then,
screaming with victory, he grabbed her hair and jerked her to
the ground where she struck her head against a rock. Startled,
the young one stared at her in confusion, and then the Crow
warrior turned back to aid Crooked Leg.

Crooked Leg, momentarily stunned by the fall from his
horse, was trying to remount when the young warrior reached
him. Despite his greater size and strength, Crooked Leg was no
match for the frenzied young Cheyenne. In an instant he was
thrown into the water. Gasping for breath he struck viciously
with his lance, and the young warrior, twisting away, turned
just in time to see a Crow brave swinging an ax at his head.
Ducking the blow, the young warrior reached out and, catching
the Crow's wrist, used the downward momentum of his swing
to propel the Crow brave down into the water. Spinning back
then, the young warrior deftly pulled away the Crow's stone ax
and with a sharp blow to the man's head sent the Crow scurry-
ing away into the world of spirits, most probably surprised at
the dramatic turn of events.

Without hesitation, the young warrior spun back and lunged
at the again attacking form of Crooked Leg, he who was re-
sponsible for the evil in the young man's life. Parrying with his
arm the strike of the older man's lance, the young warrior
boldly threw himself at the suddenly frightened Crooked Leg.
For a long moment they struggled, and to the two remaining
Crow warriors it seemed that the greater size and strength of
Crooked Leg would bring them victory. But a sudden twist, a
punishing blow, and then a scream that became, at the end, a
gurgle from beneath the water, sent Crooked Leg wandering
aimlessly along his dark road to the west.

Slowly standing then the young warrior turned to face the
two remaining Crows. For an instant they hesitated, and at that
moment young Grey Hawk broke from the bushes, running
toward his fallen mother. With a howl of rage and frustration
the young Crow with the maimed eye spun his mount and
darted after the child, snatched him up, and galloped into the
trees, his companion following closely behind.

Instantly the young warrior was in pursuit, but his naked feet were no match for the quick start and rapid pace of the horses. At last, exhausted, he turned back to find his young son, Smiling Wolf, holding his mother's head in his tiny arms.

Desperately the young warrior pulled the still form of Tashina from Smiling Wolf and into his arms, and then gently he caressed her face and whispered to her. But it was no use, for Tashina, the companion of his childhood, the sweetheart of his dreams, and the mother of his sons, was dead. She had been sent, at the hands of the disfigured Crow, into the world of spirits, into the star nations above.

My sons, the old man said softly,
this man wept
bitter tears,
and lifted a mighty prayer to
the great Creator.
But His ears were closed, and
Tashina
remained without life.
    Many seasons have come
and gone, and
this man
has lived much with
loneliness.
In this loneliness he has often asked
why? Why was such a thing
allowed
to happen?
He still does not know,
and so has determined
that the ways of
Wanken tanka
are not meant to be
understood.

What about Grey Hawk? Spotted Deer asked. *What happened to him?*

The old man, his eyes closed, took several deep breaths as

though he were in great pain, and the boys were about to go
for their mother when he again spoke.

    Pain and anger and sorrow, he continued,
burn holes in
the covering
of a man's
heart,
letting his life
drip away
needlessly.
    For many seasons this man
searched for his
lost son,
losing those seasons and
forgetting
that the other son,
Smiling Wolf,
had need of his father, also.
    One time only this warrior
came close,
holding his lost son briefly, and
giving him
the quilled amulet,
much like the amulet
your father now
wears.
But then the river was
too swift,
the night too dark, and the Crows
too many.
In battle this old man lost
once more the brother
of your father,
and has not
seen
him since.
    For many seasons this man
has waited for

Man Above
to hear his pleas.
But now he has no more
strength
to wait . . .
Perhaps this is a good day
to die . . .

There was a sudden spasm of coughing, and then with a long sigh the old man fell back against his willow backrest. Twice his chest heaved, and then with a shudder he lay still. The boys, frightened, backed slowly from the sweat-lodge. Once outside, they turned and ran into the howling blizzard, fleeing as one toward the sanctuary of their mother.

For the women, for the three small children, and for the man who would soon return empty-handed from his hunt, it was a time for sadness, a time for loneliness, a time for preparing the burial scaffold.

Part Three

First Encounter

The winter wind whistled softly as it slid icy particles of snow across the hastily built scaffold. The sun, hidden behind the grey of the winter storm, gave no warmth, and its muted light made the burial of the old man seem even more melancholy to his family.

In reverent silence the son, Smiling Wolf, lifted his pipe in a prayer and an offering to the Great Creator, tears of loss and loneliness streaming down his cheeks. For a brief moment then the stillness was broken as the women trilled their grief and respect in the time-honored tradition of their people.

Slowly the family mounted their horses and moved down off the ridge, leaving the body of the old man alone with the snow and the softly sighing wind.

Down they rode then, down off the ridge and across the meadow, forcing their horses into the wind as they made their way slowly through the deepening snow toward the abandoned encampment. It was a time now for mourning, a time for wandering, with the great Cheyenne warrior, Smiling Wolf, leading out as the new patriarch of his family.

Unknown to the family, however, their time of mourning for the old man was to be short-lived. For high on the ridge across the valley a pair of cunning eyes, well hidden, excitedly watched their approach.

Ducking quickly back out of sight, the elated young Crow scout, one of a party of six renegade warriors returning from a rare winter raid, mounted his horse and rode rapidly down to where his five comrades were waiting. Gesturing with his hands, the scout quickly apprised the men of his discovery, their numbers, their strength, and of the white horse their leader rode.

Their Crow leader, an older man with a badly deformed eye, made a quick decision. They would attack! Instantly another of the warriors argued that an attack in such a storm would be unwise. He, however, was voted down with looks of scorn and derision. Quickly their booty was stashed, war paint was applied, and the six Crow braves cautiously made their way to the crest of the ridge. Once there, the remaining five braves cautiously crept forward to finally gaze down upon the women and children and the magnificent horse their leader rode.

For a moment they were still, and then the scout, youngest of the party, grinned excitedly and indicated that they should attack immediately, that his longing for a woman was great. The others laughed quietly, and one drew his finger across his throat, indicating what he thought such a woman as rode below would do to a young Crow. Again all chuckled, and they became silent, watching the family slowly move toward them.

The snow, starting again, was falling heavily, and the wind was pushing it in blinding curtains before Smiling Wolf and his family. Huddling more deeply into their robes, the small group rode slowly forward, unaware of the danger hidden before them.

Suddenly the white war-horse lifted its head, its ears forward and its nostrils flared. Smiling Wolf, instantly alert, strained to see through the blinding snow. But it was no use. The falling snow was too heavy, and . . .

There! Through the swirling whiteness human shapes suddenly materialized, human shapes where none should have been. Turning to shout a warning, Smiling Wolf saw the form of a Crow urging his horse toward Dancing Moon. Hastily loosing an arrow that toppled the Crow from his horse, Smiling Wolf turned, attempting to meet the oncoming charge of still another of his enemies.

For a few moments the fighting was intense, though the only sounds rising above the wind were those of little Happy Wind crying, her older brothers yelling, an occasional grunt from one or another of the combatants, and the steady whapping of axes and lances against shields and bodies. The Crows, intent first on horses and second on scalps, were surprised at the intense resistance they encountered, not only from the warrior, Smiling Wolf, but from his women and children as well.

It became quickly evident to the Cheyenne that two of the Crow warriors were by far the most dangerous. The first had a badly disfigured eye, and the other, he who had initially disagreed with the attack, was a strangely familiar man who wore a red porcupine headdress. After the initial contact, however, the man with the headdress seemed to hang back so that Smiling Wolf found himself in a heated battle with him of the disfigured eye. Back and forth the awful battle raged. Smiling Wolf was only dimly aware that his family had scattered into the trees, and that his war-horse had also disappeared, leading two Crows after it. Wanting desperately to protect his family, Smiling Wolf concentrated solely on the hideous warrior before him.

Duck and parry, thrust and jab, slowly Smiling Wolf gained the advantage. Suddenly, though, the Crow feinted, and Smiling Wolf, deceived, found himself pinned beneath the swiftly descending serrated knife of his opponent. Desperately he reached up, caught the corded wrist of the Crow, and then with a violent twist threw him over into the snow. Pressing his advantage, the Cheyenne warrior leaped onto the still floundering form of the Crow, and with skill born of desperation brought his chipped point ever nearer the throat of him with the evil eye.

For an eternally long moment they struggled in silence, Smiling Wolf gazing down into the hatred of the Crow brave's eyes. But then, as if from nowhere, a searing pain smashed into the neck of the Cheyenne warrior. Twisting, he caught a glimpse of the Crow who had delivered the blow, and then he felt himself falling . . . falling . . .

For a time he knew only darkness, though occasionally he had a moment of faint awareness when he would realize that he still struggled forward, crashing through snowdrifts and across partially frozen streams. His family, he had to get to his family . . .

Dimly, Smiling Wolf became aware that someone was pulling at him, tugging . . . Desperately he fought, trying to get away, trying to defend his . . . The women? Was it his . . . ?

Dancing Moon and Little Feather did their best to quiet the frenzied movements of their delirious husband. If he shouted too loudly the Crow warriors who were searching through the storm would find them all. It had been only the will of Wanken tanka that they had found their husband at all. But they had, he was badly wounded, and if any of them were to survive the storm they had to get him to shelter. Frantically they dragged him through the snow, the two little boys and Happy Wind doing their best to help.

At last they came to an old deadfall beneath some large pines, and into that natural shelter they dragged the semiconscious Smiling Wolf.

Around them the wind howled, and the two women hunkered deeper into the snow and their robes, doing their best to keep the children, their husband, and themselves from freezing. Occasionally the sounds of the ongoing search would come to their ears, and they would hear one or another of the Crow braves shout an order or swear an oath of vengeance. But the Great Man Above was smiling upon them, and for a time even their tracks were hidden by the storm.

Suddenly, however, there was a sharp crack of breaking brush, and the family looked up into the penetrating eyes of the Crow with the red headdress. For a long moment none of them moved, but then the Crow reached for his ax and the children cowered back in fear while the women prepared to defend their husband to the end.

But then a strange look came over the Crow warrior's face, a look that to Dancing Moon seemed somehow familiar. Long he gazed into the eyes of the terrified family, thinking deeply about something. For a moment he turned away, and then he looked

back, staring intently at them. Then, without hesitation, he
thrust his ax back into its place, turned his horse's head, and
rode silently away into the storm.

The women, not understanding, gazed openmouthed into the
swirling whiteness where the Crow had disappeared. Then, as if
by command, a gust of wind-driven snow swirled about them,
and the necessity for warmth and survival caused them to forget
all else, even the unheard-of behavior of the strange Crow
warrior.

Part Four

The Scaffold

Through the mists of failing eyesight and in total desperation the old man struggled against the cords which held him bound. In an agony of aching limbs he twisted his emaciated body back and forth, back and forth, straining with all of the strength of a great spirit against an unseen enemy which would not release its hold.

And as his old body fought, so too did his mind, fighting through a choking, strangling fear of the unknown in the hope of finding understanding.

Oh, how he wished for his hands, his friends, the warriors of his soul! Yet they were bound, anchored at his sides; and try as he would he could not work them loose.

In frustration and pain and fear he struggled, and as he fought, the first tears started from his aging eyes and flowed down the creases of his skin where they mingled with the water from the melting snow.

And so that much he knew. It was snowing, he was bound tightly within a buffalo robe, and he was not within the lodge of his son, Smiling Wolf, the lodge where he had been when last he remembered.

Sheetshe! he cried aloud as he twisted his leathery face away from the icy blasts. This was bad! Very bad! Could this be what it was like in the land of the Sky People? But if it were, and he were there, then where were the deep blue skies, the green hills with bright streams wandering between them, the vast herds of buffalo, and the sacred hoops, the lodges of his people? And if he were there, why was the wind so cold against his face?

Another icy blast raked across the old man's shivering frame, and as it subsided he could hear the whisperings of the snow drifting along the ground below, swirling around the small piles of rocks that supported the poles of the scaffold.

Scaffold! Could it be?

Yes, it had to be!

He was on the scaffold of the dead! And now the old man grunted in shock and fear as sudden memory swept across his mind.

It had been his day to die, the day that he had looked forward to and yet had feared for so many long seasons. He had sung his song of farewell for those few who might have cared to listen, and then he had lain back to await his departure into the west, into the land of the Sky People where the black road of his troubles was to end.

The old man thought for a moment, wondering how he could have been so wrong. He had thought he was on that road, he had thought that he was about to walk away on the wind. It was obvious that others too felt him dead. Thus he was on the scaffold. Yet he was not dead, but was in fact very much alive, and now he must determine what to do.

Hoka-hey! he suddenly shouted into the wind, grinning widely as he shouted.
Hoka-hey, Grandfather!
This is a good joke you have
played.
A very good joke.
You have played many, but this
is the best, and

the old man who lies on this scaffold
salutes you.

For a moment he paused, wondering if the Great Wanken tanka, the great God, the one he called Grandfather, could even hear with the wind howling so loudly. Yet the cry of the wind should not stop the ears of Wanken tanka, no, not even a fierce wind like this one. He would hear, and now this great but painful joke would come to an end.

Grandfather,
though you do not feel it, the wind here
is cold,
and bound as this body which you have created is
to this scaffold,
it is unable to build a fire for
warmth.
Therefore, let us end this joke,
that this old man who wishes
to die
may continue his journey
to the west.
These eyes are slowly
fading,
these ears are good for little except getting
cold,
these fingers ache and are no longer
nimble,
and these feet move more slowly than the season of
hunger.
Grandfather,
the weight of many winters is upon
this old back,
and it is in this man who lies before you to say,
this is a good day
to die.

Expectantly then, the old man closed his eyes and straightened his chin, and for many minutes not a single muscle on his aching body moved. But death did not come — no, would not come — not even when it was so greatly desired. So after a little time the old man grunted in an agony of cold and began struggling once more.

Straining hard against the leather thongs that bound him, he continued the excruciating ordeal of trying to work his arms free. He would breathe deeply and then exhale all the air he possibly could, using the tiny space his hollow chest created as a place to move his arms. For many long moments he strained against the rawhide cords, and though the pain was great, he did his best to conceal even from himself his knowledge of the agony he felt.

At last, however, he was forced to stop. The cords were wrapped too tightly around his shoulders, he could not work his arms beyond that point, and the pain made further movement almost unbearable.

Ah, Grandfather, he groaned, trying to soothe his burning lungs and aching arms.
Give this old man the strength to free
his limbs;
either that, or free his
spirit.

Then he lay still, thinking. His bones were brittle, and he had to be careful about them. Still, if he was going to get to the ground, he had little choice. He was going to have to . . .

Suddenly his breath stilled. At first he wanted to doubt his old ears, to wipe out the memory of the sound he heard. But then it came again, a lonely, eerie howling that was at once a part of the wind and yet distinct from it. Almost instantly the cry was taken up from another quarter, and now the old man knew.

With terror mounting in his chest he waited, and moments later, when the sound came again, he was certain that it was nearer, much nearer.

Desperately the old man looked upward, and he was about to plead with the Great One again when he saw, gazing at him

from the swirling clouds, the face of his beloved Tashina.
Startled, he cried out to her.

Tashina!
My Tashina . . .
Do you come for
this old man?
Is it time
to walk . . . ?

But then, just as suddenly as she appeared, the vision was
gone. The old man found himself alone once more, alone with
the cold, the snow, and the howling on the wind.

Now, in an agony of heart that was so much more than cold
and pain, he began to tense and untense the muscles in his body,
straining back and forth, leaning with all his will first one way
and then another. In a short time the scaffold crashed to the
ground and the old man convulsed in pain, his breath driven
from his chest when he hit.

Sheetshe, Mother Earth, he gasped, struggling desperately
for air, *when last we touched,*
your
breast was soft,
moist, and pliable
as a mother's breast is
to her
children.
But now this old man feels only
your bones,
hard and unyielding, cold and
cruel.
Have you then
joined
with Old Man Winter,
and the hunger of the wolves,
to make this
battle

more difficult?
Dho! One hopes not!
This old body hurts too much
already.

Desperately he sucked in breath after breath, trying to straighten out his decrepit and timeworn body that screamed in agony with each movement. Yet the howling of the wolves made his fear overcome even the pain, and it was not many moments before he pulled himself with a great heaving from the bound-up buffalo robe and collapsed scaffold. Gasping and trembling then from both fear and cold, he began a frenzied effort to free the half-frozen robe.

Under the best of conditions it would have been painful work for his age-bound fingers, but with snow and ice frozen into the hide he soon felt himself to be in a kind of endless agony. Because his sight was blurred with icy tears, he was forced to rely on feeling, and the cold of the wind was so intense that he quickly lost any semblance of that. And to make matters worse, the howling on the wind was getting ever closer.

Grandfather, he wailed in desperation, his hands beating a tattoo against his thighs in an effort to restore circulation.

O Great Wanken tanka,
once already this old man has explained that
the weight of his winters is heavy
upon him,
and his old bones
creak
in the cold.
His fingers are not able to free
this robe,
and his spirit longs to slip from
his withered frame.
Why is it,
then,
that he must live?
May he not just lie back
and die?

The old man, still fumbling with the cords and poles of the scaffold, paused in his wailing to listen again to the fearful message on the wind. Oh, how the howlings of those wolves terrified him! If only his eyes would once again clear that he might stand and do battle! But he could not see clearly to fight, and he knew that if the wolves found him he would be at the mercy of their savage hunger. He had seen such a battle once, and the memory of it would never leave him.

O Great Wanken tanka,
where is the strength
of this old warrior?
Time has robbed him of this,
and now do you expect him
to battle
without it?
Sheetshe! That is bad!
Can you not give him back
years?
Where is the
justice
this warrior has heard of
so often?

Yes, he thought, and the icy wind made things even worse, for his withered body was now so cold that he had little control over it, little control at all. How could an old man like he . . .

Grandfather! he wailed once more, shouting into the wind in an effort to build his courage,
Old Man Winter
has blown in on his cloud
from the north
and has bedded down on the
mountaintops,
covering them with his robes of
snow.
His ice-bound fingers
have reached down onto the hill
where this old man sits,

stealing away the life from his
limbs
and holding all he touches in
his grip of death.
His breath is roaring from
his lips,
pelting
Mother Earth with
snow,
making her soft brown soil hard,
like the rocks,
and soon he will curl up and go to
sleep,
drawing all things into himself,
all things but the
cold
and the wolves.
Grandfather,
this old man who sits before you
has seen,
already,
more snows and more grasses than a man
should see.
His eyes are long dead,
his ears are not as they
should be.
His limbs shake even when he has done
no work,
and pain gnaws at them continually.
His only purpose seems to be
consuming food,
food that he can no longer .
provide
for himself,
food that a dutiful son
must provide.
You see, Grandfather,
this old creature is but a
burden, a burden upon

the life of his
son.
To the wives of his son he is only
more work,
and to their children he is
nothing,
nothing at all.
*   O Mighty One,*
let this old body nourish
Mother Earth!
Let this spirit
walk up on the wind into the land
of the Sky People.
O Great Wanken tanka,
do you hear?

In answer the winds howled more fiercely than ever around the hilltop, and now the old man's body began to shake even more violently with the cold. As long as he could he sat in silence, his boney old shoulders hunched against the wind, but suddenly he sat up with a start, listening. He could hear them again, he could hear their hungry cries blowing past him. Once more he clawed at the frozen robe, knowing he needed its warmth, yet fearing to work any longer trying to obtain it. The wolves were nearer, much nearer, and already he seemed to feel their razor-sharp fangs tearing at his flesh.

In terror he struggled to his feet, turning first one way and then another, straining to hear the wolves, straining to know if . . .

And then his foot slipped on an icy rock and he fell heavily, awkwardly, into the snow. Desperately he lunged to his feet once more, turning to run, and as he did so he tripped and again fell to the earth, striking his forehead painfully against the rocks that had supported the scaffold.

O Great God, he wailed through the screaming wind, doing his best to control his pent-up emotions.
Why? Why must
an old man

suffer so?
All his days this man has
feared death,
and now on the day when
courage to die has finally
come,
death has blown away on
the wind,
leaving him
alone
to suffer
once more.
Sheetshe, O Great One,
if you wish this
weary old man to
die,
then let it be quickly,
and not by his
brothers
the wolves
or by Old Man Winter.
If you wish him to
live,
then . . .

And the old man, crawling forward in the snow, suddenly saw with his feeble eyes the shaft of his war lance, the lance he had so carefully crafted many seasons before.

With a feeling of wonder he grasped it and pulled it to him, and then he sat running his fingers back and forth along the chipped stone point, thinking deeply as he did so.

Ah, Great Man Above, he finally murmured,
is this the way it is
to be?
Do you show this old
creation
the lance
that he might do battle?

Dho, one hopes not!
One does not battle
on top of the mountain
of his years.
Yet the lance is here,
and this tired old warrior
wonders how . . .

And then another blast of wind and snow slammed against the old man, hitting with such force that he was almost toppled over. Hastily he turned and ducked his head, doing his best to avoid the icy fury of the storm. And as he did so he felt before him the frozen buffalo robe he had abandoned only moments before.

For an instant there was no comprehension, then with a look of awe he lifted his wrinkled face to the sky.

Grandfather,
This old person has angered you.
That was not his
intention,
and he feels great
regret.
You have shown him his lance —
and now the robe.
His body shakes even more with the
cold,
which is the way his body chooses
to tell him that he is being
an old fool, and that he
must get busy.
Grandfather,
this man finds it a clear
and happy thought,
thinking that you have used his
old body
once again to teach him, as you have so often
before, with happiness and pleasure,
sorrow and

pain,
the lessons you would have him
learn.

Quickly then the old man set about cutting the bonds which held the robe. His lance, chipped to a fine serrated edge, cut the thongs easily, and so the man moved rapidly from cord to cord, wondering as he worked that God should want him to remain alive.

The wind still slammed furiously against him, and the snow flew before it, drifting into ridges and sifting into and through any opening its seeking and probing fingers could find.

Yet the old man closed his mind against the biting teeth of the snow, steeling his body against it as he forced himself to think of nothing except freeing the robe and then fleeing before the wind. And the howling of the wolves came to his ears again, now close, now far away, but always there, always there.

Terror gripped his spirit as he redoubled his efforts to cut the robe free, furiously sawing while his mind darted rapidly from the wolves to wonderment about his life and back to the wolves.

Suddenly the robe pulled loose, and instantly the old man was on his feet and moving across the top of the hill, the robe held behind to protect him from the pounding of the wind.

And as he stumbled forward he prayed into the wind, his prayers more random snatches of thought than organized supplications. Yet prayers they were, of questions not understood and of fears not under control.

O Great One,
this person is old,
and his people have
no idea
what a dying old warrior
is good for.
Sheetshe!
Neither has he.
Yet he wishes to learn.
Grandfather,

we both understand that this old body
can do very little
any more.
But maybe to be needed a man
does not have to do
something.
Maybe he can just be there,
like a star in the nations above,
for others to take
their direction
from.
Is that to be the purpose of
this old man?
If so, then he is willing.

    But, Grandfather, he added, doing his best to smile,
this old man you have created would ask a favor,
very small.
When a fire glows it does so because
of warmth.
If you wish this creation of yours
to glow,
then perhaps you will
hold back his brothers
the wolves
and help him
get warm.

Once more he wondered how such an old one as he could be
expected to do anything. What more could there possibly be?
What could be left to learn? What could be left to do? What
could . . .

One other favor, O Great One.
When it is time,
will you tell this old man why?

Part Five

The Cave

With tottering steps the old man anxiously made his way down the steep slope of the hill, keenly aware of the nearness of the wolves. The snow, only a foot deep, was just high enough to cover most of the rocks. And these, with their icy surfaces, proved most treacherous.

In his haste his feet slipped constantly, and often he slammed heavily into the drifting snow. After several such falls, as he was climbing shakily to his feet, he paused with sudden realization. Then, with a feeling of awe, he lifted his face once more to the snow-shrouded sky.

Grandfather,
this man is humbled again by your
constant kindness,
and his old heart beats with
gratitude.
You help this body move by making it
so cold

that it must. And then,
knowing that old legs are frail
and shake with age,
you, O Wise One, provide the snow
to soften their
falling.

And so, with the wind and the snow swirling around him, the old Indian gripped the almost-useless buffalo robe tightly and continued groping his way to the bottom of the hill. Often he fell, and not infrequently he suffered severe pain as his boney legs slammed against a rock or his head against a low-hanging tree limb. Yet he forced himself to ignore the agony as he pushed forward, ever forward, trying desperately to catch a glimpse of his departed family as he fled from the hunger of the howling wolves.

Though it was impossible to tell with any certainty, because of the intensity of the storm, the old warrior had the feeling that he was in the same valley where his son and the rest of the village had placed their lodges. But if that were true, he wondered, then in which direction must he go to find them?

In the lee of a lightning-blasted pine he paused to rub the numbness out of his body, catch his breath, and consider his choices. He could hear the stream directly before him, and he knew that he could now go in either direction and have an equal chance of finding his people. And perhaps the sacred hoop of lodges would still be there. Yet within his heart the old man feared that all of the people, including his family, would be gone. He knew from long years the customs and the traditions of his people, and he knew as well as they did that it was never wise to remain long in a place of death. As well, his own family would have begun their wandering so that they might mourn his passing in a proper manner.

O Great Wanken tanka, he groaned aloud,
how we have all
been fooled!
What is the purpose in
this, that this old man is dead to all

but himself?
Would it not have been
better
if the bones of his youth
had been scattered about on
the prairie
to show where a warrior
had fallen,
and to make a story?
    Grandfather,
this man has tried, but as yet
he cannot see
where it is good ·
to grow old.

For several moments the old man rested against the tree, staring out into the snow-filled valley. Suddenly, there before him, he saw once more the face of Tashina. But before he could call out, her face had gone, and he was gazing into the sunlit meadow where first she had told him that she was to have a child. Dropping from his shoulders the deer he had killed, he had knelt down and, placing his ear against the woman's already-swelling belly, had tried to hear the sounds of his child. No . . . children; for now the old man could see Tashina lying in the lodge with his two newborn sons squealing on her lap. The vision was so real that the old man started to reach for his sons, only to have them fade away and dissolve with the face of Tashina pleading with him to hurry. Then she too was gone, and the old man found himself gazing once more into the silent valley, wondering, wondering . . .

The wind had now grown quiet enough that he could hear the whispering of the snow as it drifted over the ground, seeking out and filling the hollows and low spots, making the whole world seem flat and smooth. The faint sound brought back memories, and for a moment or so he was in another time, another place.

    The snow is so
beautiful, O Great One.

How could this old man have forgotten
how beautiful
it is? See how it turns
the meadow grass
into giant eagle feathers,
and bends the pines low
in humility
with its weight.
*   Out there some geese are flying past,*
late on their journey.
Do you hear?
Though these old eyes
cannot see them clearly now,
they have seen, through the
seasons,
many such, and they know,
O Great One,
that the sky is the same
color
as the underside of their wings.
*   Ah, Grandfather,*
could anything be more beautiful,
more pure?
Do you show this beauty
to cause an old man
to wonder
how he can bear to die
and leave this lovely creation?
Dho! Of course you do!
Like the pines, this man is
bent low, in humility,
and it is a good feeling
to have.
The snow has made all things
white
and clean. Perhaps
it will do the same
for him.

Onward then he struggled, on through the freezing, drifting
snow. Oh, how his legs ached! They were trembling so badly
that he wondered how he could go any farther, any farther at
all. And his chest. He had never felt such burning pain! Would
it ever end? Could he ever stop? It had been some time since he
had heard the sound of the wolves, but the old warrior knew
that meant little. They were behind him. Yes, and they were still
hungry.

Sheetshe, he groaned as he pushed himself through a clump of
trees he had stumbled into,
since the eyes of this old warrior
have dimmed
he has never ventured
far alone
upon any path,
no matter how familiar.
   How, Grandfather, can he expect
to flee when there is
no path, no,
nor no strength to
find one.
   Dho —

And the aged warrior suddenly cried out as he stumbled over
an old windfall and tumbled into the snow, a jagged branch
slashing through his leggings and into his thigh. It was several
breaths before the man realized what had happened. But when
he saw the warm blood trickling down his leg and into the snow
he panicked, hacking frantically at the buffalo robe, fearing not
so much the wound as that the smell of blood, his blood, would
drive the wolves into a killing frenzy. In an agony of fear he tied
a strip of hide about his thigh, struggled to his feet, and fled.
   The man heard no sound as he moved, no sound but the
swishing of his feet through the snow. That, and the murmur of
the nearly frozen stream, the crying of the wind in the pines,
and yes, he was sure he could hear the howling on the wind
once again.
   He was out of the trees now, almost running as he moved
across a gradually sloping meadow. Constantly the meadow-

grass tugged at his ankles and feet, and tiny ice crystals tore like knives at his leggings and moccasins, gradually cutting thin the finely tanned leather from which they had been made.

O Grandfather, he groaned, as he stumbled forward,
do not let these brothers
the wolves
scent the blood-smell
of this old man.
 Do not let them . . .

Often now he put snow in his mouth, soothing with its coolness his tortured lungs and throat, and as well as he could he held snow against his wound, hoping the cold would slow the bleeding. Yes, and . . .

With a grunt of surprise the old man toppled over a bank, and as he smashed through the ice and into the freezing water of a beaver pond he felt his breath driven from him in a rush of bunching muscles, muscles constricted by the freezing water.

For a moment he was certain he would drown, but then he realized that the water was not deep. Struggling to his feet he pushed his way to the bank and pulled himself out of the icy pond.

Now his tired old body was shaking violently, and he could never remember being so cold or feeling so lost and so alone.

O Great One, he sobbed as he struggled to his feet, wringing as much freezing water as possible from his leather clothing,
why,
why is this old man
suffering
when he has traveled
so far
along the dark road
of his troubles?
Does there not come
a time
when one has
suffered
enough?

What good can come of
such suffering
now?
Does there not come
a time
when the dark road
ends?
When a man
at last
finds happiness
and peace?
You gave this man the lance,
O Great One,
that he might
live.
Yet you also allowed him
to stumble
and feel all over his frame
the icy grip of
the stream, an icy grip
that will bring death
quickly
on a day such as this.
There is also the
blood, warm from
the wound
in his leg,
and now, no doubt,
flowing too from these
old feet
where the moccasins
have worn away.
In what better way
could a warrior
leave
a trail
for his brothers
the wolves?

> *O Grandfather,*
> *what would you have*
> *this son of yours do?*
> *Yes, and where*
> *would you have*
> *him go?*
> *His mind longs for*
> *death*
> *and yet fears it as greatly*
> *as his frame must.*
> *For though his legs are tired*
> *and feeble,*
> *and shake with the cold,*
> *yet they fight on,*
> *carrying him forward.*
> *This old warrior is unable to walk*
> *as fast as he once did,*
> *or as far,*
> *but he can walk,*
> *and still does.*
> *Why is it that*
> *his legs, his arms,*
> *his feet, his hands,*
> *and his mind*
> *continue to fight*
> *on and on*
> *against death,*
> *when it should be*
> *so welcome,*
> *so pleasant?*

Through the afternoon the old warrior made his way slowly and painfully through the grass and snow and over the rocks of the valley floor, moving constantly to keep warm and to escape the wolves, searching in vain for something that he might recognize, some sign that the lodges of his people were near. Though the snow had stopped falling and the wind was less violent, the sky was still overcast and threatening, and the old man could feel the chill of the storm upon his cheek. Soon, he knew, he would have to find shelter, he would have to find warmth.

The whispering stillness was profound, and he found himself fighting a growing sense of loneliness. Yet now it was there, and to ease its haunting pain he spent more and more of the afternoon discussing his thoughts vocally with his God, the Great Creator, the first Father, Wanken tanka. In all his life the old warrior had never spoken so directly nor so frequently to this great Being, always viewing himself as unworthy to do so. But now, somehow, all that had changed. He had been on his way, he felt, to the land of spirits, and then for some reason had been called back. That seemed to give him the right to initiate communication. And so, as he stumbled forward through the afternoon, he spoke with his quiet and quavering voice of the thoughts that plucked at his mind, and of the feelings and fears that brushed against his heart, sharing himself and thinking more deeply than ever he had before.

As he made his way through the snow, he was amazed that he could be so cold, so nearly dead, his body in such agony, and yet have his mind wander backward along the pathways of his life the way it was doing. Those pathways, he knew, had been rarely trod, and then not for many seasons. Yet now he walked them easily, and he wondered at it.

He thought of the days of his youth when his arrows found the life of the fleet antelope and of the high-climbing sheep. He thought of sitting within his lodge as he watched his mother prepare the *wasna* from the buffalo his father had killed. He felt again the stirrings within his breast as he first gazed upon Tashina, the young woman who would be his wife. And he recalled the heaviness of spirit, the totally helpless feeling that had been his as he held her lifeless body against his chest. Oh, the loneliness of that day! The bitter irony of life, that one so young could never know the joys of a full life. Even now, after such a long time, he felt the tears start in his eyes as he thought of the heartache that had been his, the loneliness that had started the moment he found her dead and broken frame, the loneliness that still continued to haunt him.

Quickly he forced his mind away from Tashina, bringing it forward to his struggles through the snow and to his freezing and starving and nearly dead old body. Intently then he strained his ears. Again he could hear nothing, nothing but the wind and the sounds of his fleeing and his labored breathing. Where were the wolves? Where was the sound of their coming? Where were —

His mind was away again, away on a long-ago war party when he had first learned of his own courage. From there he thought again of Tashina and of how many horses he had given to finally win her. On and on his thoughts drifted, going back and forth over the years as though the seasons did not exist at all, as though all time were the same and it was all one day.

Grandfather, he murmured,
how is it that
so many seasons have
flown by,
passing so quickly
across this man's
life,
almost without his being
aware
of their going?
When he takes a drink
at the stream,
the face gazing at him
from out of the water
is a stranger to him.
That face is wrinkled and creased.
It shows a stooped old man, one who must use
three legs.
He has on his head
the white warbonnet,
hair as white as the winter snow,
thinning
until there is almost not enough of it
to braid.

O Great One,
this man sees this image in his mind and he knows
it is himself, yet at the same time his spirit
cries out,
Wait!
That wrinkled frame is not him at all,
but is instead simply a
prison,
a clay prison within which the young man
that he is
struggles for release.
And, Grandfather,
most interesting of all
is how this man feels.
He knows he is
what others call
old,
for he has seen many winters
pass him by.
Yet somehow
he feels no different than he did
that clear morning when he first leaped,
unaided,
to the back of his buffalo runner.
His heart, his spirit,
is the same now
as it was then.
Though his eyes do not see well,
his heart still leaps with joy
when it sees in memory his beautiful
woman,
or hears her voice,
or feels her softness.
It thrills when it recalls the sun
burning the clouds in the afternoon
sky.
It still cries with sorrow
when it hears needless
pain

or learns of
senseless brutality.
It still beats with wonder
as it observes the birth of a
child,
or the rebirth of Mother Earth as she greens
to life
when the time of cold is past.
    What this man who stands before you is saying,
O Great One,
is that he always thought,
when he was young,
that he would feel old when he reached
thirty winters,
of fifty winters,
or even eighty winters.
Strangely, now that he has passed even these,
he does not feel old at all.

Here he paused for a moment, grinning a little, then he continued.

He should say, Grandfather,
that he does not feel old
until his bones
begin to ache with
the cold.
Then he feels old!
Still, this old frame within which
he dwells
is his friend
and does its best
to keep up with him.
There have been many times
when he has not treated it
well,
yet it has forgiven him
of a great deal.
He should not be so unhappy

with it.
When the children of his son, Smiling Wolf,
look away with contempt,
or pity,
then he should say, Do not worry,
old friend.
They do not understand the
battles
you have fought daily
for so many long seasons.
Soon, though, they will understand,
for age comes
to all, even children,
one sunrise at a time.
And it will come to them,
each of them,
with as much
surprise
and swiftness
as it came to you.
Dho, yes, when
one recalls—

Suddenly across the old man's senses swarmed the haunting, chilling sound of the wolves, much nearer. And the man knew their cries were different, too, the sound was more excited, more full of anticipation. They had found his trail! They had found the blood from his wound.

O Great Man above, he cried in agony and terror, *do not let these brothers the wolves . . .*

And he thought suddenly of the day he sat on the side of a hill watching a pack of wolves hunting below him. They had found a moose, a strong young male, and he watched in amazement and not a little awe as they circled it, taking turns feigning an attack while they wore down the strength of the helpless animal. Then, as if on some prearranged signal, two of the wolves leaped for its head, distracting the attention of the moose. And in that instant of distraction another wolf leaped in behind and slashed the hamstrings on the moose's hind legs, totally crippling it. From that instant it had been only a matter of time, only a game that the wolves were playing, only . . .

In a frenzy of fear the old man floundered forward through the snow, pushing, praying, pleading. Only . . .

Again came the lonesome howling, so close now. So close. Almost instantly he heard a series of short coughs and growls, and with a chilling realization the old warrior knew it would do no good to run any farther. Far better to stand and face them, doing battle as best he could, making the price they paid for his life as dear to them as possible.

Quickly then he rose to his feet and turned, holding his lance out before him, facing them. Strangely, now that the wolves had found him he felt no animosity toward them, no enmity at all. They were simply animals, hungry brothers doing all they could to survive.

Dho, Brothers, he shouted, doing his best to keep his fear from leaping into his voice.
Of all the things this old man has wished
to consider,
the thoughts of your hunger
were not among them.

Loudly he began to sing his courage song, lifting his feet slowly up and down as he pointed the lance first one way, then another, turning slowly in a circle as he tried to tell from which direction the attack would come.

And now his thoughts flew off once more, flying back to a time of struggle when his grandfather had counseled him.

My son,
a true man must learn to be
many things at
many times.
Often he will have need
for fierceness,
like our brother the bear.

But just as often he will have need
for gentleness,
like our sister the
butterfly.
There will be times when he must be
as a mountain,
straight and tall,
his eyes seeing everywhere
at once.
But there will also be times
when he must be
as a valley,
silent and blind to all.
And there will always be times,
hard times,
when a man should be as an eagle.
Then he can mount the wind,
higher and higher,
until he suddenly sees
how small
everything truly is.
Then he can smile and
return,
and things won't seem so hard.
Then he can . . .

And in that instant the wolves rushed, silently and yet so
swiftly that the old warrior had no time to think, no time to prepare except to lift his lance a little higher as he saw them
coming.

He was first hit from behind and knocked forward. As he fell
he thrust his lance forward and felt it strike flesh. Then something like hot fire took hold of his arm and he was down and
rolling in the snow and there were warm bodies and he was
thrusting and swinging with his lance and kicking and the foul
smell of the wolves was almost more than he could bear.

He wondered as he struggled that he felt no pain, for he could
hear their teeth snapping and knew that at least one of the

wolves was tearing at his leg. He was also aware that in his twisting and fighting the buffalo robe had become wrapped around him. With sudden realization he understood that the robe had, by covering his head and neck, probably saved his life. And as that thought flashed through his mind he felt the robe savagely yanked from him. Desperately he pulled himself around, groping for the lost robe, reaching. Suddenly a wolf's body was across his face and he screamed and shoved at it with his empty hand, pushing with all his might, and then his foot found another one and suddenly he was alone.

For an instant he lay still, listening to the savage growling and fighting that was going on near him. What had happened? Somehow for the moment they had lost him. The wolves were fighting over something else, and he was alone. And then he saw. The robe! Of course! The robe had his blood on it, and the wolves must have become confused about what they were after! Instantly the man began to pull himself through the snow, trying to get away from them, still fighting for his life even when part of his mind kept telling him how hopeless it was.

Before him was a fallen log, its ancient branches reaching up to block his way. In an agony of fear he pushed his way through them, thrusting his lance before him as he dragged himself over the rotting tree, getting as far away as possible, getting . . .

And now there was another windfall, another tree in his way. As he pushed his body over that one he heard the rush of feet and felt the fangs tear through his leggings and into his leg.

Instantly he lashed out with his other foot and shoved against the wolf, and then he was over the other log and rolling and . . .

Suddenly he felt the snow give way beneath him. Wildly he reached out, grabbing, but there was nothing to hold to and he fell, landing heavily in soft earth several feet below.

For a moment he lay still, listening to the savage snarling directly above him. But suddenly it ended in yelps that sounded like fear to him, and then he was alone again, staring into the inky blackness. Slowly, gradually, he became aware that the air around him was warmer, that he was out of the wind, and that he was not so alone as he thought.

With his old heart in his throat he whispered a greeting, but when several queries brought no response, he began to inch his way toward the sounds he heard, the sounds of heavy breathing.

He crawled very cautiously, yet even then he froze in terror when his hand rested not on earth but on a fur-covered body. And he would have fled instantly had his old legs been able to support him or had there been anywhere to flee to.

As it was, the shock of the experience was more than his drained and aged body could tolerate, and the old man fainted dead away, his chilled body slumping to the earth next to the hibernating grizzly his groping fingers had found.

Part Six

The Grizzly

Much time passed before the old man at last opened his eyes. For a long moment he stared into the darkness, trying to understand where he was. Oh, how he ached! Every bone and muscle throbbed with a will of its own, and he could never remember being so sore. Then realization flooded upon him and he hurriedly began inching away from the warm body against which he had been lying.

Moments later he was as far away from the giant bear as he could get—no more than four or five steps—and he was even more aware of the precariousness of his situation. Though his eyes could see little, his probing fingers quickly told him that he was in a cave that was not so much a cave as it was an overhanging bank supported by the roots of a great tree. Across that overhang several other trees had fallen, the years had deposited leaves and other debris, the storm had laid down between two and three feet of snow, and now the whole mass formed a very effective cave indeed. Despite his groping search, the man could find no way out except for the small hole, now mostly covered, through which he had fallen. And try as he would, and as desperately as he wanted to, he could not muster the strength to leap up to the hole.

With a feeling of stark terror gripping his heart, he faced the sleeping bear. Somehow he knew that it was large, even for a grizzly. Also, for some reason he was certain that it was a male. The bear seemed to be sleeping soundly, yet still the old man huddled against the dirt bank as far from it as he could get. Of all his four-footed brothers, this one only did he truly fear, and this one he feared with all his heart.

Many times during his long life he had felt fear, but always before he had only to recall the vision of his youth and touch the sacred bundle hung around his neck and that fear would be gone. Then he would be full of power and courage, signs of the true man. But now he felt no power, no courage, only the cold hand of fear clenched around his entrails, the cold hand that had gripped him constantly since he had awakened on the scaffold.

Over and over he touched the sacred bundle, but always when he sent his thoughts back to his vision they would somehow get lost and wander over to the willows along the stream where he and his sons were playing games. What a clear day that had been, with the sun warm upon the earth and the willows thick and green with new leaves! The stream was singing a new song, a song of joy, and he sang with it, for never had he felt so alive. At first they had wrestled, he and the boys, and then each disappeared into the willows to see who could capture the other. It was almost instantly that he heard the screaming. Terrified, he turned and rushed through the heavy growth toward the sound. Suddenly he burst into a tiny clearing and there he found his son, Grey Hawk, groaning in agony. The giant grizzly quickly brushed aside his tiny son and charged, and as though it were only one sun ago he could feel the white-hot slash as a monstrous paw raked his ribs, sending him reeling into the willows. Then with a searing and crushing pain he felt the powerful jaws close upon his shoulder and lift him into the air. From that time he had known nothing until the day he opened his eyes within his lodge to gaze into the face of Tashina, the one who was his woman.

For years he had lived that experience over and over in his dreams, and now the terrible wounds that were in his mind had opened once more. How, he wondered, could he be expected to go through all that again?

Then, just as the light faded from the cave and the sun sank into the earth, the bear stirred. For a moment or so it snorted and grunted, and then it rolled over to its other side where it finally settled down again.

The old man, terror-stricken, cowered against the dirt bank, and it was not until his senses began reeling that he realized he was holding his breath. Slowly he exhaled, carefully struggling to do it as silently as possible. For some reason the bear stirred around several times during the next few hours, and each grunt and movement drove a new flood of terror over the old man.

Before dawn, sick, exhausted, and fearing that his end was near, he finally dozed off. Suddenly he was no longer in the cave, he was no longer a crippled old man, and it was no longer the moon of dark red calves. Instead he was a youth and it was the moon when cherry stones hardened, and he was standing with his body painted all over in the sacred color of red, and he was trembling with fear and exhaustion. For three days, from sunrise to the time of its setting, he had danced the sun dance, blinding himself as he stared into the sun each day as it slowly trailed across the sky. Now he was quaking with fear as the holy man sliced his breasts and inserted the leather thongs he was supposed to slowly tear himself away from. At first he felt no pain, but as the drums began and he leaned back with their rhythm against the thongs, all the pain in the world seemed to center upon his breasts. He forgot about the dance, he forgot about his desire for a vision, he forgot about everything but the pain. It felt like someone was pulling the raw heart out of his chest. He wanted to cry out and drop to the earth and die, but somehow he found the strength to dance, to dance and to keep on dancing.

This seemed always, only suddenly it was not and the world had gone dark. He was spinning, spinning and falling, and it was so dark, with nothing he could hold to. And now he felt again the fear knot up in his belly as he fell around and around, down and down.

And this too seemed always until it wasn't and he was no longer falling. He was still spinning, but he was suddenly in the form of a hoop, rolling on and on, over many grasses and over many snows, all alone in a wide, flat world. Still he felt the fear, and now with it the pain came again, agonizing and overpowering, constant and burning, driving his heart into his throat until he thought he would die with it.

Then suddenly he was not alone, but was rolling beside another hoop, this one bathed in a pure white light. As he saw the other hoop his pain and fear vanished and he felt a calmness, a calmness so total and so complete that he realized instantly who the clear hoop was. The clear and sacred hoop was the Grandfather, the Great Wanken tanka, the God of all, who had come to travel with him.

On they traveled, on and on, and it seemed there was no end to the seasons they crossed. Occasionally they would start to separate, and each time that happened the pain and fear would return. Pleading he would call to the Grandfather, who would come close again, driving the pain and the fear away.

When this had happened many times, the man began to wonder why it was so, and as the wonder formed a thought in his mind, the clear sacred hoop vanished and a red eagle appeared, sailing down to land in a tree against which he himself stopped rolling.

Quietly then the eagle, who was once again Wanken tanka, spoke, teaching him the meaning of the sacred hoop or circle, a meaning which the warrior had never remembered. Many more things did the eagle teach him, but of these only one could the young dancer recall.

My son, the eagle said,
the life of a man is a happy
time,
but it is also a time
to suffer and endure.
Pain is able to teach
courage,
and without courage there is nothing
good.

In times of fear and pain
the proud heart
dies,
and then the power of Wanken tanka
will come in
and live in that heart,
giving it the true courage that
fears nothing,
seeks not for praise,
and strives for the good of
all.
Give many thanks for fear and pain.
They are friends, and
they will be yours often,
often enough
that you will become
the man
you are to be.

Slowly the old man regained his senses, listening with one ear to the movements of the bear as he thought of his dream, of the dream he had now known twice. The dream was strong, full of power, and now as he thought about it he felt his body filling with the old strength, strength such as he felt in the dream whenever the clear sacred hoop that was Wanken tanka came near.

Ah, Grandfather,
when this man was a youth he was taught
that there would be many
hard things,
but that of them all, four would be
the hardest.
Getting food was the first,
for without food
there is nothing else.
The second hardest thing would be
losing his oldest son.
The third hardest thing would be

losing
his woman,
and the fourth hardest thing would be
fighting a big war party
when his own was small.
Over the years,
O Great One,
this old man has known all of these.
And they are indeed hard.
Yet none of them is so hard as the battle
he fights now
to overcome the fear in his belly,
the fear that cripples.
These others he has done alone,
using the strength he has found
within himself.
But this fear
is more than he is,
and without you he is lost
to it.
Grandfather,
in the days of his youth you gave this man
a dream
and taught him this truth,
that without you, he is
nothing.
Now he has walked many roads,
some that were good,
some that were bad,
and he has passed over many
grasses
and many
snows.
He wears the white warbonnet,
his body is stooped and bent,
many of his teeth have been uprooted,
his eyes are dimmed,
and he must walk with three legs.
Is it not strange that in

the winter of his life
he must be called back from
the world of spirits
that he might learn again
this same truth?

For some time the man was silent, deep in thought. Daylight slowly crept into the hole and felt its way about the cave, and still the old man did not move. The bear stirred once more, grunting a little, and the man seemed to pay it no mind. And then suddenly a grin spread across his wrinkled old face, and his eyes once again began to twinkle.

Very well, Grandfather,
this old man is beginning to find understanding.
Because he no longer hears so well
with his ears,
he is now learning to hear
with his heart,
and he finds that a clear and happy thought.
All things are directed by you,
O Great One,
for the good of your creations —
the two-footers,
the four-footers,
and all the wings of the air.
The older this man grows the more he understands
that we are all
brothers and sisters,
children of Maka,
the Mother Earth.
Our frames come from her,
and one day each of us
must return
our frames to her,
that we might more easily
travel
into the world of spirits,
where we will find

true happiness.
This is a thing that all hearts
desire greatly,
for the land of spirits is
a pleasant
and beautiful
place.
   Yet, Grandfather,
you have taught that we all come here
with a purpose.
In your wisdom you have made a man
so that he will not
enter
into the world of spirits
until his purpose is
fulfilled.
If the air he breathes is
shut off,
he fights for more.
If he feels hunger or thirst
he searches until that need
is satisfied.
If he is set upon by an enemy,
he fights
with great strength
and determination
that he might preserve his
life.
   This man's own life has crossed over
many seasons,
and lately he has longed for the world
of spirits
where Tashina
and all the friends of his youth
now dwell.
   Yes, O Great One,
this man mightily dislikes
loneliness
and the pain it brings.

Yet he feels there must be more
to his life here, for he
clings to it
so desperately.
    All his life has been a dance, a dance
and a song.
When he was young and
light upon the earth, his steps were quick
and easy.
Now he is heavy upon the earth, and
his steps are slow, halting
and difficult.
But his dance is still strong within him, and
still he sings his song.
His song is of the air
he breathes,
his song is of the memory of the great boulders
in his life,
his song is what he hears and feels
in his heart,
his song insists
that he will never die.
    And now his old frame too sings
a song,
an aching song of
wounds untended,
an aching song of hunger.
You see how he is clinging to life?
It is not the season for berries;
this man has no wasna and no papa,
nor has he a lodge
with the juicy hump of a fat buffalo cow
roasting
on the fire.
Yet, Grandfather,
there lies a brother,
the bear,
sleeping and awaiting his entry
into

the world of spirits.
On him there is much meat,
and his coat will easily keep an old man
warm.
This man sees now, with his heart, that it was no
accident
that brought him to
this den.
Be close to this old warrior, therefore,
that he might have
the courage to do what must be
done.

Carefully then the old man felt around on the underside of the trees until he found shreds of the soft inner bark of the cotton-wood. This he worked with his hands until he was satisfied it was right. Next he took snow and cleaned the wounds on his arm and leg, and then he bound the bark to them with what was left of his leggings.

Now he felt around until he found his lance, which he had somehow pulled into the den with him as he fell. The point had broken during the fall, so the old man patiently began chipping a new edge on it. He did not hurry because he could not, for all his speed had fled with his youth. Yet he worked well, and when at last he was finished he wondered that he should have done such a fine job when he might never use it again. Still, all things had a life of their own. He had enjoyed a strong frame. Should not his lance have the same joy?

Cautiously then the old man prepared to slay his brother, the bear. He had no sacred pipe, so he held his hands as though the pipe was there, offering prayers to the four quarters of the earth and to Wanken tanka and to Maka, the mother of all. At last he made as if to set it down, stem toward where he felt the sunrise would be, dedicating it to Wanken tanka. Next he gave thanks to the grizzly, thanking it for its warmth, its courage, its strength, and its life. Then he felt with his fingers for the right spot on the bear. Now he was ready.

For a moment he stood still, calming his trembling limbs that perhaps did not yet know that he felt no fear. Then with all his strength he cried out, *Hoka-hey!* and drove his lance deep behind the left foreleg of the bear, seeking its heart.

At first the bear only grunted, but suddenly it lunged to its feet, and with a mighty roar it stood swaying back and forth. The old man, backing slowly away, stared in amazement as the giant grizzly growled in pain and anger while it stood batting at the lance in its side. Then with another roar it attacked the old tree, fiercely shredding the bark and wood with its claws. Suddenly it fell back to the earth, driving the lance in even deeper. Again it stood to attack the tree, and again it fell back against the lance. Now the roaring was a continuous thing and in the midst of it the bear suddenly turned and began dragging itself straight toward the old man.

For an instant the warrior's heart leaped into his throat, but then before him he saw in his mind the clear sacred hoop that was Wanken tanka, and suddenly his fear was gone. Quietly he stood and faced the roaring grizzly, which slowly dragged its huge mass to where its swaying head was within inches of the man's chest.

The stench of its breath was fearsome, and blood and saliva flowed from its mouth into the old man's tattered leggings and moccasins. Its huge mouth was open wide, and its teeth, yellowed and filthy, were larger than the aged warrior could have ever imagined.

There was a scream of terror in his throat, for the stench of the bear was full of evil memories, and he knew that he had to run, to flee. Yet somehow he kept his old feet firmly planted and knew that no sound escaped from between his lips.

Grandfather, he suddenly heard himself whispering, amid the fearsome roarings of the bear,
for the first time this man is
thankful
that his eyes do not
see well
and that his ears do not
hear well,
for even now this old man
is seeing and hearing more

than one can comfortably
enjoy.

For an everlastingly long time the bear roared in his face, only inches away and yet coming no closer. But life gradually left it and it sank to the floor of the cave where at last it was still. After many more moments the man carefully located his lance and removed it, and with its point he took the strong parts from within the bear, the favorite parts. These he ate raw, chewing each mouthful thoroughly. His long fast caused him to fill quickly, and when he could eat no more he lay back and slept. Upon awakening he ate again, and then he began the laborious task of removing the pelt.

Part Seven

The Search

In the midst of the howling blizzard the five remaining Crow warriors, carrying their dead companion, limped into a thick stand of pines where they took shelter. There was little discussion as a fire was kindled and they crowded around for warmth. After a time, when chilled limbs were once again working and minds were not so numb, each of the warriors took a handful of pemican, dried and pounded buffalo meat mixed with fat and berries, and slowly ate. Then, and only then, did they discuss the battle with the Cheyenne known as Smiling Wolf.

As they talked, it was evident that all the Crow warriors held their leader, he of the disfigured eye, in great fear and admiration. All, that is, except the Crow with the sacred red headdress. While the others boasted loudly of past deeds, he quietly contemplated, and when the others declared with arrogance their intentions during a future encounter with the Cheyenne family, he looked silently away. Finally his noninvolvement became obvious, and when questioned he declared boldly that in his opinion the attack had been a mistake. Further, any future assaults would only compound the problem. The best thing they could do, he felt, was to take their dead brother and return with all haste to the lodges of their people, leaving Smiling Wolf and his family as though they had never existed.

At that, the leader, his face radiating a vicious cruelty, leaped to his feet.

Woman! he shouted, thrusting his finger at the other Crow. For a moment the two stood then, eye to eye, the one's face filled with disgust, the other's with an unreasoning hatred. The leader then began to declare, venomously, how he personally would have the blood and the life of the Cheyenne, no matter what the cost.

As the other three braves stood watching, awed into silence by the ferocity of him of the disfigured eye, the Crow with the red headdress stepped quietly backward, held a small stick forward, and broke it before his leader. There was a momentary gasp from the three onlookers, for all knew their companion had, by his simple action, declared his contempt for their leader and his severance from anything led by him.

Haughtily, he of the disfigured eye turned and walked away, and after a moment the others followed. Quickly they were given orders for the continuing search, and then mounting, they rode away, leaving the resolute warrior standing alone by the fire.

For hours the Crow warriors searched for the family, once even coming within a few feet of finding them, only to have a covey of quail explode from the bushes and divert them away. At last the four split up, and it was shortly after that when two of the warriors, crossing a meadow, came upon the blood-stained tracks of the old man. Mistaking them for the sign of the wounded Smiling Wolf, the two set off along the trail, eagerly anticipating the glory they would receive when they came upon him.

When they came upon the spoor of the wolves they were first surprised and then concerned, for there was no honor to be found in a dead enemy. Suddenly, amidst some large rocks, the footprints of the wounded warrior disappeared into a large hole in the snow. The two Crows quickly looked around, saw no wolves, and then cautiously crept into the mouth of the cave.

Satisfied, after a hasty glance, that the body of a man lay on the floor, the two Crows climbed outside, where one departed to notify his companions while the other remained on guard.

He had not been alone long when from out of the cave issued the wildest and most ferocious sounds the Crow had ever heard. Alarmed, he leaped to his feet, uncertain of what should be done. The sounds then grew louder, and the brave, suddenly not very brave, turned and, stumbling and falling in his haste, beat a rapid and frantic departure.

Some time later, as he squatted trembling, alone beneath a tree, he heard a strange shuffling sound. Glancing up, he saw, not thirty feet away, the head of a giant bear moving behind a low hummock of snow. His head filled with visions of evil spirits, the Crow fled desperately away, never even learning that beneath the bear hide labored the tired, worn-down frame of the old man.

Still later, when his companions returned to the site of the cave, they were astonished beyond measure to find the skinned and partially butchered carcass of the giant bear. Knowing only of the severity of Smiling Wolf's wounds, and assuming that it had been he in the cave, the three Crow warriors rode away with the beginning of true respect growing in their hearts. Later, when their erstwhile companion at last joined them, telling a tale such as they had never before heard, that respect changed rapidly to awe and fear. Yet pride drove them on, and the search continued.

Part Eight

The Family

For endless time the old man staggered onward. He was so exhausted that he soon lost all sense of time, of direction, of motion. His stumbling forward was simply reflex action, the result of a great heart bending a feeble old body to its will.

At last, however, even reflexes gave out, and the old man collapsed into the snow.

O Great One, he moaned softly,
this man has tried,
but in these
legs
there is no more
strength.
In this heart
the will has
died,
and it is in him
to say once more,

this is a good day
to die.
This is . . .

Suddenly he stopped. There before him, her face glowing
with radiant youthfulness, stood his Tashina. Her eyes, wide
and dark as the pools in the stream beyond their lodge, were
filled with tears, and with them she beckoned . . . beckoned . . .

And then she was gone and he was running through the trees.
He was naked, or nearly so, and the thick shrubbery tore at his
flesh. He had to hurry, to hurry faster, but he couldn't, and he
felt himself falling farther back, farther back . . .

Before him now knelt the boy, Smiling Wolf, a woman's
head cradled in his small arms, his face streaked with tears of
anguish.

Sheetshe, he shouted, trying to draw nearer, trying desperately to reach his son. But then the boy was gone and he was in
the woods again, still running but getting farther away rather
than closer. Desperately he ran, but just as he was about to drop
from exhaustion he was no longer running. He was no longer . . .

Tashina! If she would only come nearer, if only she was not
crying, not beckoning with her eyes . . .

As the old man's senses returned he gradually became aware
of another presence. Yonder, somewhere close, was a horse. He
could hear nothing, see nothing, yet his nose told him that it
was there, and he could not doubt that.

Straining his eyes to see more clearly, the animal suddenly
came into focus, standing atop a nearby hummock of snow.
Cautiously then he crawled toward it. Then he paused, and
after many moments of waiting he hesitantly approached,
worrying about his enemies, the Crow. Only after long
moments of careful searching was he sure that the horse was
alone, for it was not mounted, and there were no other tracks in
the snow.

Only then did he look carefully at the horse, and suddenly, at
last, he recognized it. It was the white war-horse. It was the
buffalo runner of his son, Smiling Wolf. For a small moment he
wondered where his son might be. But that thought was swept

away by gratitude, by great thanksgiving that his son's horse
had come to him during a time of such need.

With a sigh of gratitude the old man looked upward. For a
moment only he remained thus, as silently a grin spread across
the aging wrinkles of his face and he struggled onto the back of
the buffalo runner.

The horse turned and looked at him, much as if it were
making certain that he was ready. Then gently it moved off
through the snow, going down the canyon, carrying the old
man forward.

The old man could not remember the last time he had felt so
good. He was horseback again, and it had been only when he
had climbed onto the back of the animal and ridden a little
that it came to him how much he had missed riding. There was
something about the feel of a good horse beneath one, something about the way its muscles moved, about the way it lifted
its feet, that gave to a man a sense of strength, a sense of well-
being.

Hoka-hey, he shouted joyfully, shaking his lance in the air
above his head,
this man gives thanks,
Grandfather,
that today is here, and that
he continues
to make
memories.

In fact, as the old warrior thought of it, he really did feel
good! The wounds from the wolves, if not healing as rapidly as
he would have liked, were still healing nicely. This day his
muscles and bones were giving him few problems, and on this
horse he suddenly felt, for the first time, that despite the slow-
ness and the feebleness of his withered frame, he could make it
back to his family. He could now return to his family.

Dho, Man Above, he continued,
what of today?
Is this warrior to have

more trials? More troubles?
As he sits atop the
mountain
of his years
is he to make
more memories?
Must he do battle again?
No, this man does not
think so.
He has slain his brother
the bear,
and so has slain also
his fear.
He does not know what you,
Grandfather,
would have him do.
Yet he is ready,
and will do it
as he can.

A little later the horse snorted and reared back a little, so the old man slid to the snow and examined the trail of several other horses. As he pulled himself back onto his horse he could see that there were either six or seven horses, all ridden, and the old man had the feeling it was a war party, though of course he could not tell from which nation they came. Yet as he rode he wondered, and the thought came again and again that they were Crows. He felt certain that the tracks had been made by the enemies of his people.

For most of the day the horse carried him forward through the silent drifts and across the bare ridges of a series of breaks that swept down and into the river bottoms. The silence was profound, and he could never remember feeling the stillness so deeply. It was as if all the earth had gone to sleep and would never awaken. For a time the old man almost felt that in all the world there was only himself and the buffalo runner, but when it suddenly snorted and wheeled around, he knew that such was not the case. Carefully he listened, straining his old ears, and then he heard the heavy panting that was now so familiar.

Dho, sheetshe, he mumbled.

The wolves were with him again!

Without hesitation he turned the horse and continued his journey, knowing that as long as they kept moving steadily the wolves would hold their distance. The old warrior did not fear them any longer, viewing them simply as brothers who were doing as their kind did to satisfy their hunger. Yet he was cautious, and he did his best to keep the horse calm while they kept a safe distance.

Late in the afternoon several deer bounded away from them down the hill, and as the old man listened he heard the wolves cry out and leave his trail in pursuit of new game. And it was shortly after that when the horse, of its own volition, suddenly turned from the trail of the Crows and climbed steadily up the crest of a wind-whipped ridge, its barren and rock-strewn surface totally unfriendly to any tracks at all.

Gradually yet steadily they climbed up through the pines and aspen until they emerged onto a flat tableland. This the horse carefully picked its way across, seeming as it did so to hide its own trail. The old man marveled and continued to let it have its head, feeling certain the horse was taking him where the Creator wanted him to go.

At dusk they came suddenly to an abrupt break, a canyon that was not visible until they were almost within it. The horse paused for a moment and then went over the edge, descending a steep game trail that entered almost immediately into a thick stand of fir and aspen.

For some time they moved steadily forward through the twilight, the old man sensing the movements of his horse carefully, noting with interest when it put its ears forward and snorted with excitement. Cautiously the aging warrior swung the horse around while he slid to the ground and once again examined the snow. He then remounted and continued, and suddenly they broke into a small clearing where stood a lodge, a solitary lodge of his people.

Slowly he rode forward, still not sure exactly what he had found, but excited by the sudden aroma. Rapidly he examined it. The tepee was in bad shape and appeared to be empty, for he could smell only the stale odor of smoke long dead. Neither was

there any recent sign of horses, nor were there any strips of
meat hanging from the bare drying rack. Yet the snow near the
doorflap was trampled, and the old man knew that someone
was inside.

He cautiously moved forward, and it was when he reached
for the opening that he first heard the singing, the soft low
strength song sung by a woman as she prepared herself for
death. Gently then the old man pulled aside the flap and stepped
inside.

He knew instantly that he had been wrong about the fire.
There was one, though it was very small, little more than coals.
There were also some occupants in the lodge. Two women sat
beyond the fire, three children huddled behind them, and beside
them on the ground lay the still form of an adult warrior.

For an instant the two women stared at the old man in
shocked disbelief, and then in terror they dropped the knives
they had been holding in readiness and cowered back with the
children, their wailing songs now becoming howlings of terror.

At first the old man did not understand why they should act
in such a manner, but when one of the women wailed his name
and spoke of ghosts, he suddenly understood what was wrong.

Standing as straight as his arthritic old bones would let him,
in dignity befitting his position, he thought for a moment about
what should be done. Out of respect, a man of the people never
spoke directly to the wives of his sons, nor they to him. If communication were needed they spoke through others. That was
the old way, and it was the good way. Still, these women were
the wives of his son, who could not talk himself. Therefore, he
must converse directly with them.

Dancing Moon, Little Feather,
do not fear.
This man is no spirit, but is still wearing
the same old wrinkled hide he
has always
worn.
It is true that he started on his journey to
the west,
but as you see,

he has been called back.
Now he is here, following many long hours
horseback.
Do you have something
to feed
an old man?

As he seated himself there was total silence within the lodge,
and then Little Feather began wailing again, singing a song of
shame and sorrow. In patience the old man listened, not understanding why these women should feel shame.

But then Dancing Moon spoke, telling him that they had no
food at all, and they had had none for nearly three days. In a
flood the story of how their husband, Smiling Wolf, had been
wounded by the Crow poured out. It had now been many hours
since they had dragged him home. He was still unconscious, and
they had been without food for all that time. Nor dared they go
far looking for any, for the Crows were still around, searching
for the great warrior, Smiling Wolf.

Silently the old man turned his back, hiding the tears of pity
which he felt for these people, his family. Grasping his lance, he
stood and shuffled out to his horse. There he removed the bear
bladder full of pounded meat, offered a silent prayer of pity and
sorrow, and then carried the meat back into the lodge. After
seating himself once more, he handed the bladder to Dancing
Moon. She took one look at it, smiled broadly, and began
preparing a meal.

The old man then examined Smiling Wolf, carefully applying
his healing arts while he instructed the women about what they
should do. The wound was very bad, and it had a foul smell to
it, a sign that made the old man wonder that his son was alive at
all.

Later as they ate, the old man listened carefully to the activi-
ties of the two women and the three children. Dancing Moon
seemed strong and eager. Little Feather sounded ill and seemed
very weak. Of the children, only Happy Wind, the little girl,
was sick, and she could hardly eat. The two boys, Spotted Deer
and Horse-that-follows, were so frail and quiet that the old man
could scarcely tell they were near.

After the meal the old man broke the long silence.

Spotted Deer,
you and Horse-that-follows saw me
coming
and came here to warn
the others.

It was more a statement than a question, and the boys, wide-eyed, nodded in agreement.

Hoka-hey! Yes you did!
You were hidden behind an aspen
which is bent as
an old man with many seasons upon
his shoulders.
Furthermore, as you turned to run,
one of you slipped,
yes, and narrowly missed going over
the cliff.

Now the boys were truly amazed, for they had told that to no one. What was even more amazing, both of them knew that the old man was nearly blind, going deaf, and mostly crippled. How, they wondered, could he have known?

And so the teaching began. The old man, as if reading their hearts, explained that by its actions his horse had shown him where they were. The slipping was there in the snow for all to see who cared to look. Even, he added with a grin, if they were all but blind and had to use their finger-eyes. Then the old man praised the lads, telling them that any men who could move that silently and that swiftly would one day be great warriors of the people.

At this both boys beamed with pride, and Horse-that-follows forgot to feel foolish about slipping in the snow, something his older brother had contemptuously chastized him for.

Men!

Warriors!

Suddenly the boys had a new respect for this old man, this

father of their father, this wrinkled warrior who wore the white warbonnet, who walked with three legs, and yet who had the strength and courage to praise two small boys for a deed well done.

Sensing that he had won the confidence of the children, the old man reached out and gathered them about him, placing Happy Wind upon his lap. Then, in the warm and quiet darkness of the lodge he began talking, telling the children a story that he had learned when very young, a story designed to teach an important lesson.

When he finished he sat quietly, listening to the silence, wondering what the reactions of the children would be.

Finally Horse-that-follows spoke, asking a question. The old man answered, another was asked, and suddenly he knew that the boys were seeing beyond his age and his ugliness, seeing into his years. They were ready to be taught.

Another story came to mind, that account brought forth another, and so he talked of his own past when the days were bright and the nights short, teaching the children through his stories of lessons and values they so much needed to know. And as he talked, Dancing Moon fed ladles of warm broth into Little Feather, Happy Wind, and then into the unconscious form of Smiling Wolf.

Some of the stories the old man told were old, so very old that even his grandfather, who had told them to him, could not tell when they were first told. Other stories he told were of things he himself had seen, of his own war parties, of the time he had killed the sacred white buffalo and had obtained its powers, and of course of the time just past when the Great Creator had given him the power to slay the giant bear.

This story fascinated the boys most of all, and even the women were silent as the old man dramatically related it detail by detail. When he had finished speaking, each in turn examined the pelt, exclaiming in awe at the long sharp claws and at the size of the giant head.

Long after the family was asleep, the old man stared into the comfortable darkness of the lodge. His thoughts seemed to ride with the wind that he knew swirled the smoke near the opening above the fire. His thoughts blew first to one thing and then to another, never following a straight pathway. He thought of old friends, of long-dead enemies, of his first real buffalo runner, of the lessons he had learned from his grandfather, and of that clear morning so long ago when he had gazed into the dawn and had suddenly, for the first time, caught a glimpse of what life was about. In a flash he had understood that he was learning great lessons each day, both because of what he did and because of what others did. If those lessons remained with him alone, he realized, they would be of little value. Shared with others, however, the lessons he had learned would help to lighten their burdens, and would become of even greater worth. All his life, therefore, he had done his best to share the thoughts of his heart and the experiences of his soul with those around him.

And now, when he had thought that all was past, he found himself teaching again, directing the lives of these people who suddenly had such a great need for him.

Ah, Grandfather, he spoke quietly into the darkness,
like the morning light
in the star nations,
perhaps this old man is at last
beginning to glow.
Hoka-hey,
did you not see the eyes of those
little boys
dance
when this man spoke of his brother
the bear?
And did you not see the glow of
their faces
when he called them
men,
when he called them
warriors?
And is it not so that we become
most quickly
who
we think we are?
Ah, Grandfather,
as you have taught this creature,
so will he teach these children,

by convincing them that they are,
in fact,
the people you and he know
they must one day
become.

And so the time passed quickly as the old man sat in the warmth of the lodge of his son, teaching the ways of a true man to the children. Whenever the weather permitted, he would have the boys walk with him along the paths near their lodge, or he would sit in front, nodding approval of the little woman-things Happy Wind was learning or of the man-feats of the two boys. In truth, the children became his ears and his feet, and never were two young boys and a little girl so anxious to please. Constantly they would run to him with news of the childish things that so delighted their fancy, and he was always as happy as he could be to hear of them. The two women wondered that an old man should get so excited over the things of children, but one day Dancing Moon suddenly found understanding, and quietly she explained to her sister-wife that it was the children the old man was excited about, not their childish things. He was making the children *feel* important, that one day they would *be* important. That was the way of a teacher, of a true man.

Many other things did the two wives discuss about the father of their husband. Now that he had returned, they both found themselves wondering a great deal about him. As Dancing Moon expressed it, the old man who was now directing their lodge had changed. He was not the same ancient warrior whom their husband had placed upon the scaffold. Neither of the women could decide exactly how he was different, how he had changed, unless it was that he seemed stronger, more sure of himself, more certain about what he was doing.

And Dancing Moon also noticed another change, a change that came from within herself. Prior to the old man's supposed death, she had only tolerated him, forcing herself to lead him around and care for him. She wasn't certain why he repulsed her so, whether it was his helplessness, his deathlike appearance, his quavering voice that moaned out of his toothless mouth, the odor of age that was about him, or simply the fact that he was so far removed from her in age, so far removed from the things she knew and the experiences she felt and enjoyed.

But now all those feelings had fled her heart, and with surprise she found herself being drawn closer and closer to him. Certainly he was still in need of much help. Obviously he still looked and acted old, older even than she could imagine. Yet now she understood that despite his age and attendant problems he was still a man. In fact, he was a man who was very similar to her stricken husband. And as she thought of him in that way he became much easier to understand. His thoughts, his feelings, and even his actions were no different from those of a young man, except perhaps that they were restricted by age. And as she thought of this, Dancing Moon suddenly understood that the father of her husband was not so far removed from her own feelings and experiences as she had thought. In fact, he probably understood more about her and the thoughts and feelings of her heart than she did about herself. And he did so because he had had longer, much longer, to feel and to think about and to understand the emotions she was just now learning to feel. Now she recalled the words she had heard him speak to her husband one evening, words that had made little sense to her at the time.

My son,
a man will never learn
all he needs to know
with just one
experience.
Experiences must pile up,
as boulders do
at the foot of the cliff
of a man's life.
And as they pile up,
each one will give him
insight
into the others,
giving him the time
he needs

to evaluate and to think
about them.
In that way only
will a man learn
the lessons
Wanken tanka
would have him learn
from the experiences
he chooses to give
him.

And now Dancing Moon understood that age, while usually handicapping an individual physically, actually gives him greater freedom and greater wisdom spiritually and mentally. It was this wisdom, this freedom, that was so visible in the old man, that was drawing her to him so strongly. No wonder he was having such an impact upon her and upon the children. No wonder she found such delight in watching and feeling the inter- action between her family and their grandfather. What a special thing it was to have him with them!

One day, on one of his walks with the boys, the old man paused to rest against a large cottonwood near their lodge. He couldn't get over the feeling of having to rely so completely upon these children and the women. Yet as he thought of it he suddenly realized that the boys were becoming much more re- sponsible, more able to help him than they had been. And then a thought came to him, a new thought, a thought that would not leave him alone.

Grandfather,
this old warrior
just thought of a new thing,
and he would
question it.
Do all things
happen
for good?
Is it good for a man
to suffer

pain, misery and
loneliness
most of
the days of his life?
  Dho, this old man
thinks maybe so.
Could it be that
all things are
good,
if not for the one who
suffers,
then at least for others who
would learn
from his suffering?
  In this man's
multitude of
years
there is much weakness,
much helplessness, and
much sorrow.
He does not enjoy this
at all.
Yet from it these
little ones
and the women
seem to be learning.
This old warrior feels,
suddenly,
that he has been selfish,
that he has not been
willing
to share
what he is
with them,
simply because he has not
enjoyed it
himself.
  O Great Creator,
give this man

courage
to live this lesson you
have just
shown him.

After a moment he called the boys to him, thanked them for leading him so carefully and so well, and then asked them to examine the tree against which he had been leaning. When they had looked carefully he asked Spotted Deer to describe the tree to him, all of it. When he was finished the old man spoke again.

My sons,
the branches of a tree in winter
are like the paths this old man has trod
in life.
They go in all directions.
Some are sturdy and have led
to much happiness.
Others, too fragile to stand, have led
to many sorrows.
Yes, this tree reaching upward to the sky,
with its bare branches tangled, is like
the paths of life.
They seemed confusing when they were taken,
for the leaves of this man's
summer
kept him from seeing clearly.
Yet now, in the bareness of his
winter,
he sees that each path,
like each branch,
had a purpose — to strengthen the roots
of his life, to help him become the man
he has become,
to help him become the man
he is to be.

That night he stood alone outside the lodge, and once more, as had happened so many times in the past, he was struck with the beauty of the night. Out in the darkness an owl hooted as it drifted down the corridors between the pines, and above him the stars glowed closely like multitudes of campfires spread out across the star nations.

   O Grandfather,
how old memories seem to flood
by,
tumbling forward out of the past like a
churning, foaming stream when the snow
has begun to melt.
It is good that the joy
of remembering
is as strong as the pain,
for that comes without warning,
slicing deeply into
one's heart.
   Walking back from here along
the pathways of the mind,
all that this man sees of his
life
are the great round rocks,
and not their jagged edges,
nor the small and unimportant
stones.
These have been ground to nothing and
washed away
by the river of time,
leaving him with nothing to remember
but good things.
   He knows that he has experienced
pain,
yet the scars have healed and are now
hidden in his
wrinkles,
much as the bark of a tree
hides its old wounds.
Where this man walked there seemed to be much of
sadness,

yet he remembers now mostly the good things —
the touch of his woman, Tashina,
the joy of victory,
the pride of riding into battle
beside a tall son.
He knows there was much on the earth to make him
unhappy,
but somehow there was never
time
to listen to the broken song
others seemed determined to sing.
There was always too much joy in
the mornings,
too much beauty in
the afternoons,
and too much softness in
the darkness.
  Grandfather,
one finds it a good thought
that he has been able to sing
a whole song
during his life.
Now his memories are mostly of
happy things, the things that have all come together
at last,
to make this, your creation, the man that
he is.
  One of the little ones, Horse-that-follows,
asked today
if this man was lonely.
He said no, because he is not,
not in the way the boy was thinking.
But you know, O Great One,
that this man is lonely, lonely for his friends
who were
and who have now taken that long journey
to the west.
And of course, he is lonely for one
special person,

his Tashina,
most of all.
But the pain of that sweet memory
is great,
and so he does not allow himself to think often
of her.
Still, some days her memory comes despite his efforts,
and it is almost like she is with him
once more.
His happiness then is great, but so is the
pain when she must leave. It is for
that reason only that he tries not to
remember her.
*   There is one thing more,*
Grandfather.
For many seasons
this man has longed for the way
things were
when others depended upon him.
He missed being in the center
of life,
for it is lonely on
its edge.
Now he sees that he
need never
have been on the edge
at all,
for always others have
needed him.
Just not in
the same
way.

And so the children learned quickly under the direction of the
old man. He gave them as much responsibility as he was able,
teaching them through their own decisions as well as his own.
As he expected, they frequently made mistakes, some of them
quite serious. Still, it was a time of happiness for them all, for
the old man showed them the humor of their errors.

Ah, Grandfather, he said later,
it seems to me that this man laughed more
when he was younger.
And it feels very good
to laugh again.
Was the earth happier when he was young?
He does not think so.
The sun woke each morning and
trailed all day to the west,
as it does today.
People were born and
people died,
and there was hunger and plenty then,
as now.
No, the earth has not changed so much,
nor the people.
It must be that
this old man has.
Do you know, Grandfather,
that as this man considers this,
the things that bother him now
gave him much laughter
when he was
young.
Sheetshe! That is bad!
Happy things
should never stop
bringing laughter.

And so the time passed. Once Spotted Deer and Horse-that-follows managed to slay a small deer, bringing food to their lodge. Later, when all had eaten their fill of roast venison, the old man spoke again.

My sons,
today you did a great thing, for you
killed the deer and
fed the hunger of
us all.

And little Happy Wind,
my daughter,
you too did well,
for you helped your mother remove the skin and
prepare the meal which
fed us.
Do not forget,
little warriors,
to thank the Great Creator
for allowing the deer its
birth
so that this day we might eat.
Touch the earth now,
each of you,
and do not forget that as the deer has gone to it,
so too one day must we follow.
The earth sings the same song today
that it sang for our fathers
when their laughter
warmed the day,
when their tears
filled up the
night.
Maka, the earth, sings a song
of hope.
Maka sings a song
of joy.
Maka rises up and laughs
at us
each time we forget how spring begins
with winter,
and how death begins
with birth.
That is a good thought, and
a happy thought also,
for we know always where
the path
of our life will one day
lead.

Earlier, under the old man's direction, preparations had been made for defense against a possible Crow attack. Now, following his instructions, the family moved their belongings into a nearby cave, a sacred place known about by very few. Then, again following the old man's directions, a large sapling was pulled down and a snare placed in the trail leading to the lodge.

It was Horse-that-follows, a day or two later, who saw the approaching Crow warrior, and it was that day also that the wolves arrived.

Quickly the family hid in the rocks and trees, stilling their breathing while they listened to the faint sounds of a horse's hooves. Suddenly the warrior appeared, and Dancing Moon, who was closest, almost gasped aloud. It was the warrior with the red headdress!

Cautiously he rode forward, hesitating every few steps to look about. It was obvious that he was nervous, but he could see nothing, could hear nothing that indicated . . .

Then on an impulse, the man withdrew his ax, kicked lightly at his horse, and moved forward once more, peering carefully ahead.

Suddenly, directly beneath his horse's front hooves, the snare was tripped and the rope snapped tight! The horse, squealing in surprise and fear, reared up and over backward, spilling its rider onto the slope below. Then it too fell, and both horse and rider slid uncontrollably down the steep mountainside to slam into some trees far below.

Dancing Moon, on her feet instantly, sped downhill toward the injured Crow, her knife out and thoughts of her nearly-dead husband filling her heart with revenge. But then, just as she was about to end the warrior's life, the old man reached her and stopped her blow.

My daughter, he said softly,
give thought to
this thing.
This man here is wounded,
Smiling Wolf, your husband, is wounded.
You and the others
care mightily for

Smiling Wolf,
and make prayers for his
recovery.
Might not a family
somewhere
feel the same for this
Crow warrior?

For a moment the woman stood thus, and then slowly she lowered her arm. Quickly the Crow was bound and transported to the cave, and then preparations were continued for the remainder of the Crows.

That night, as they sat in the cave, the old man felt the eyes of the captured Crow resting upon him. Turning, he watched the warrior for some time, wondering at the feeling of compassion he had for the young warrior. He was not alone in that, either, for little Happy Wind fed him of her own food several times. It was obvious that she too cared about the trussed-up captive.

And there was something else, too; something vaguely familiar about him which the old man did not understand. It was almost as if . . . as if . . . But the thought would not come, and so the old man turned away. Still, he was aware of the gaze of the captive going from him to his son and back again, though through politeness he did his best to ignore the rude stares of the Crow.

He, himself, looked at his son, however, and he found himself longing for him.

Oh, for his strength, his courage, his skill in battle. Oh, that he would arise and be well again. Gladly would the old man have traded places with him. But such thinking was folly, he knew, and so was time wasted. He must think only of the Crows, and of how he and the children might stop them. His thinking, that and the courage of two boys, a girl, and two women, was certainly not much with which to stop a war party of Crows.

It was long after dark when all the preparations had been completed and tried out, and it was a very tired group who gathered around the fire to eat. Carefully the old man examined the faces of these people, his people. There was much

good within them, and he felt a sense of pride that the children, and in a sense the women, sprang from his loins.

Yet in their faces he could also feel fear, a fear that he knew
might cripple more than a wound. He thought then of the
wolves, his vision, and of the death of his brother the great
bear, and with that thought in mind he began to speak.

When this man was young he knew
very little.
Although he was big and thought himself
a man, he had never
grown
in the way a true man
must grow.
So one day he vowed
a dance
to the sun.
That is the way of our people,
and we do it
that we might gain strength
and bring good
upon us.
The pain was worse than a man
can say,
and his mouth opened
to cry out,
but the wind came and
blew
the sound away.
Each day for three days
his eyes followed the tracks of
the sun
as it trailed across
the sky,
seeing but not seeing,
and finally the sun
blinded
his ignorance.
Each day his hands

grasped
the sacred sage and the
sacred rattle,
but they had never learned to truly
feel,
and so at last they died.
Each day his ears
listened
to the music of the
sacred drums,
but they had never learned to truly
hear,
and so at last they were
drowned
in a roaring sound.
All this continued until this man was reduced to
nothing.
And then the Creator awakened him.
Speak the truth, said Wanken tanka.
The wind blew back his voice and
the man admitted
he was afraid.
See the reason, said the Creator.
The sun gave him back his vision and
he saw all things changing,
including himself.
Feel truly sacred things, said the Great One.
His hands came to life and he held
his children
in his arms.
Hear true music, said the Creator.
The roaring left his ears
and he heard
his people
laughing.
Do you know what you are? asked
Wanken tanka,
and he said,
At last I am a man.

My sons,
change is a part of being
a man,
but most men resist it,
and fear.
Yet when we hear, see
and feel
true things,
as a man should,
then great courage comes from the Creator,
which puts all fear
behind.
Then is a man truly happy.
This is what this old man has learned.

Quietly tiny flames licked up the sides of the logs in the small fire, their flickering tongues casting dancing images of the occupants of the tepee on its buffalo-hide walls. Outside the wind picked up, and a few flakes from a new snowstorm drifted through the smoke opening.

It was at that moment that a wolf raised its spine-tingling cry out in the timber. A little later another lifted its lonely voice from a different direction, and the old man knew that his hungry brothers were back again.

Softly he directed that the horse be brought within the lodge, and then they were all silent once more, thinking their thoughts as they listened to the sounds of the wolves and of the growing storm. At last they slept, and while they did the snow fell, and the rising wind whipped it into long drifts. Slowly their tracks, and even the landmarks, disappeared, and the world became changed. The wind howled and those lesser killers, the savage timber wolves, burrowed deep under the boughs of an old pine and hid to wait out the storm, one with belly half-filled, one nearly starving. But there would be nothing for either of them to eat until the storm was over, and they knew it. For during the storm nothing moved, nothing but the wind — the wind, the snow, and the Crows.

Part Nine

The Battle

With daylight came the Crows, not noisily and with war whoops, but stealthily, as if they were trying to remain in harmony with the silent, snow-filled canyon. The occupants of the cave were certain of their nearness only when the horse suddenly lifted its head, its attitude one of rapt attention.

Earlier, long before the light from the new day had begun to color the sky, the family had been awake. From small comments the old man knew that Spotted Deer was terrified, perhaps even more than the others. Gently he placed a wrinkled hand on the boy's shoulder and squeezed, softly reminding him of the love and strength they had found within their family. He also reminded him of the knowledge they had that the Great Creator, Wanken tanka, was over all and would see that all things worked out for their good.

Now, my family, he continued,
*today we will indeed
fight the Crows.*

This man has lived long enough to learn that
fighting
is not always a good way.
But he has also lived long enough
to understand
that a man must protect the family
the Great Wanken tanka has
given him.

    But Grandfather, Spotted Deer interrupted, *if we were to go*
unarmed to them and explain that our father is far along the
road to the west and that there are no other warriors among
us—

    My son, the old man spoke quietly,
this man is happy that you
desire peace, for that is
the way of
a true man.
Yet you should understand that
hunters such as these like nothing
better
than to see
the hunted
come walking to them
unarmed.
One cannot submit
to evil
without encouraging evil
to grow.
Each time a man gives up
a principle,
each time he allows
evil
to destroy what he knows
is right
or good,
he is saying to evil,
This man supports you.

Sadly, greed and thirst for
power
are never
satisfied.
There is always hunger for more.
Hopefully there may come
a time
when men of
all nations
will lose this hunger and
this thirst.
Perhaps then they will be
more willing to
listen
and to trust
one another.
But there will never come
a time
when a man should compromise
himself
or his beliefs
endeavoring to gain such trust.
That is what evil
would desire.
And such compromise is wrong.
Always!
That is why a
true warrior
will rise above his fear
and do battle.
That is why
this day
we must fight.
  Now, they are many, while
we are few. And so we know that
the battle
will not be easy.
Perhaps the Crows will
overpower us,

and if that is to be so, today
will be a very good day
to die.
Do you understand?
    Do you understand that
today every living thing is in agreement
with us?
Today our memories are of
happy things.
Today we think evil of
no one.
Today the earth shines in
our eyes.
Today we know we defend
the right.
Today we feel no pain,
only happiness.
Today our lodge is filled
with laughter.
Most important, however,
today we are surrounded by
our family,
our courageous family.
Today would indeed be a good day
to die.

Timidly then, little Spotted Deer looked up at the old man and asked if he didn't fear death, even a little.

Ah, my son, he replied after a moment's thought,
death is a thing
that is always with
a man,
from the hour of his birth
until after he draws
his final
breath.
Only then does death cease
to be a part
of life.

To a youth death seems
an enemy,
one to be feared.
But as the days of
his life
flee past,
he learns that enemies are,
in reality,
friends,
for they teach him great lessons
about himself,
lessons that must be learned.
So too with death.
    In the winter of a man's life
the lonely wind of death
drifts quietly down
out of the darkening
sky,
bearing on its
icy breath
the snowy remnants
of autumn's last
rain.
And with a quiet sighing
it tugs
at his hair,
gently
encouraging him,
lifting him
to his tottering
feet.
Then for just
a moment
he hears,
once more,
the singing of the wind
in the trees,
and feels the wonder of
new snow held in childish
hands.

Before him he sees,
as he
has daily for
years,
the face of his
woman, smiling
the same way she smiled
on their first night
together.
It has been good,
this life.
But like the
wind
and his woman
it has flown by,
leaving him old and lonely,
wrinkled and
cold,
with nowhere to go, nowhere
but onward.
*   It is then,*
my son,
that death becomes a
welcome guest,
welcome at last because
a man finally sees
that death is not
the end,
but is instead simply
a continuing step in
his life.

Smiling then, the old man added a final thought.

Yet, my children,
this old man does not think that today
is the day
when death will come, at least
for us.

Softly then he called the two women to him. To Little Feather he handed Happy Wind, the tiny girl who had cuddled on his lap so often since his return. To Dancing Moon, the strongest of heart, he gave merely his smile and a soft pat on the arm. Somehow he knew how she would respond this day.

Next he placed his hands upon the two boys, fiercely painted—as much to give them courage as to frighten the Crows. Oh, if only their father could awaken to see them! He then reminded them of where they were to be and of what they were to do, and each boy spoke gravely and with understanding.

Finally he offered a prayer of gratitude and supplication, and then he sent the boys out into the dawning, toward their destiny.

And what a day that was! Yes, and what stories would be made that day! In long years to come, multitudes of the people would sit around their fires at night and speak of the battle fought by the feeble old man as he sat within his lodge, gaining victory over his enemies through the strength of two small boys and a courageous warrior-woman.

Laughter would ring as the storyteller spoke of the snares and of the ice slide that the boys, under the old man's direction, had built. The slide led to the cliff edge, and down its steep and slippery surface one of the Crows made an unexpected departure when he was led onto it by a small, apparently fleeing, warrior.

Pride would show as the speaker told of how a warrior of only six summers, along with one of eight summers, counted coup on a live enemy, and of the warrior-woman who all alone wounded a Crow brave, and then in a showing of true courage cared for his and the old man's wounds.

Looks of awe would encompass their faces as the listeners heard of the Crow who dived beneath the boughs of a large pine to make an ambush, only to find that he was sharing space with two near-starved timber wolves. What a noise there must have been as all three boiled out of the snow, flew over the ridge and right onto the icy slide (almost as if it had been planned) where they quickly disappeared.

Amazement would show as they heard of the hole chopped in the surface of a frozen lake through which a Crow brave and his horse plunged after being led there by a small warrior on the run.

And finally, laughter would peal out once more as the teller would relate how the two boy-warriors and their warrior-mother, knowing that nothing could be done, simply turned their backs upon the tumultuous noise leaping up from beneath the cliff, leaving Crows and wolves to work things out below as best they were able.

Ah, what a day that was, and what stories were made that day!

Part Ten

The Windwalker

The serrated, wind-whipped ridge lifted its boney back high above the valley of the sacred cave, seeming to grow by steps progressively nearer to the star nations above. There, beneath a lightning-blasted pine, the Crow with the disfigured eye stared balefully down into the rapidly darkening valley. He was alone, for of all the Crow warriors who had followed him, he alone had escaped. Now it was he alone who must seek revenge for his people.

For many long and chilling moments he sat astride his buffalo runner, his thoughts drifting from his warriors to a great white war-horse to an old man to a wounded Cheyenne known as Smiling Wolf. Over and over he asked himself how it had happened, how one who had enjoyed so much success as he had enjoyed could have encountered such trouble, such tragedy. The whole thing seemed evil, seemed . . . yes, seemed magic! They were not fighting men down below; they were fighting devils!

Suddenly the Crow understood, and so turning his mount he rode to a level place where there was little snow, dismounted, and began preparations.

When the sun appeared again he would be ready. His sacrifices would be completed, his offerings made, and he would be ready to face, in a final battle, the devil-men below.

A little later, as the old man stood outside the cave, the two boys breathlessly told him of the lone Crow warrior they had seen making medicine on the ridge high above. The old man nodded, sent them into the cave, and then stood for a moment longer, gazing into the darkness.

Giver-of-life, he said softly,
each day this man grows more
lonely,
each day he feels the
earth
to find it a little
harder.
Each day the sights and sounds
of his life grow
more dim,
each day his old heart aches
a little more for
Tashina.
Ah, Grandfather,
is it not yet time?

Quietly then he turned and entered the cave, where he took the position of honor near the fire. Carefully then he explained to his family about what the Crow was doing, how he was making spiritual preparations for what could be his final battle. The old man then told them that because his son, Smiling Wolf, could not do battle, it would be his honor to represent his family in such a way.

Weakly then the wounded Cheyenne rolled over and struggled to his feet, doing his best to declare that it was he who should do battle against the Crow. Hesitantly he stepped forward, but after only two steps he fell awkwardly onto the robe beneath him. Instantly the women and children were at his side, but weakly he waved them away, all but Spotted Deer, his oldest son. Carefully then he pulled a quilled amulet from around his neck and with great dignity placed it upon his son, charging him to aid his grandfather in his battle.

When the amulet was placed around the boy's neck, the captive Crow, who had been watching and listening intently, suddenly started. Then he looked more carefully at Smiling Wolf, whose face, for the first time, was fully in the light of the fire. Had the family been paying attention they would have seen the expression on the captive's face change from one of wonder to one of almost total hatred and disgust. Now, more than at any time since he had been taken captive, he wanted to be free, to be shed of his bonds. Quickly his eyes darted around the cave, coming at last to rest on a stone knife which had been carelessly left nearby. Carefully, while the old man talked, the Crow began inching his way toward it, moving a little, pausing, listening, moving a little more. On his mind now was only one thought—he *must* escape!

The old man, meanwhile, was thoroughly enjoying his family, knowing that with daylight he must face the Crow, from which battle he would most definitely begin his long road to the west. His son, Smiling Wolf, was beginning to recover, the women were happy, the boys were full of questions, and little Happy Wind was on his lap tickling his chin. And as she did that, the old man was suddenly aware of a new thought, a thought in his mind that seemed to say over and over, here is why.

Here is why!

Each man learns love as he gives of himself to others, and this gift he gives to them, they too must one day share, thus learning love themselves. That was the truth of the sacred hoop or circle, taught him by the red eagle of his vision, Wanken tanka, and it is the ultimate purpose of life. It is all for love!

And as that thought darted back and forth across the pathways of his mind, a smile creased his wrinkled face, a smile so wide that for a time even his pains vanished.

Following their evening meal little Happy Wind took her place again on his lap, and the old man told them a happy story,

a story of a coyote and the bright star of the star nations which
glows with happiness just at dusk.

When he was through and all were laughing in merriment, he
suddenly found himself doubled over with a knot of pain in his
belly that was bigger than anything he had ever encountered.
For long and agonizing moments he endured in silence, patiently
bearing the humility of having his family see him rendered thus.
At length, when he was able, he sat erect and spoke again.

Now, my children, this man feels
that the time has come
to tell you another
story,
a story about dying.
It too is a happy story, and
should not make you
sad.
   Many seasons ago, when winter was coming,
this man found himself alone
one day
in the forest.
It was a beautiful day,
and his soul sang as he
beheld
the brilliant color the sun gave
the leaves of the maples, a color
more beautiful than a man can ever describe.
   As he drank from the stream, he saw
that it danced
slowly over
the rocks,
making a song of
ending.
   The creatures, too, the four-footers
and the wings of the air,
were themselves singing a
slow song,
telling this man
that they too understood the

song
of ending.
Many of them were dancing
their last dance,
and the quiet music of the stream and
the gentle voice of the wind
made beautiful music
while they prepared
for death.
*   Yet there was no fear nor sadness,*
not in the golden leaves,
not in the stream
nor among the creatures
who were preparing for
Old Man Winter,
for all was as it should be,
and had been,
and would be,
always.
You see, winter is the season of
death,
and nature does not fight against it.
She simply prepares for it.
Thus, when it comes time to die,
there is happiness,
for all creatures understand
that death is not
the end.
They know that
the sacred circle of new life begins with
the death
of the old one.
*   Do you see?*
Old leaves fall and nourish the ground that
new leaves might spring forth
in strength.
Creatures too nourish the earth
as they die,
their spirits drifting away to

the west
on the night
wind.
And old men die that
young men might take their places,
learning the joys that old men
have known.
Thus there is happiness
everywhere,
here, and in the world
of spirits.
    And so as this man moved through the forest,
he saw that there was much getting ready,
much rejoicing,
and much in the way of the last dance.
    Much later, when the season of cold
had passed,
this man walked once more
through
the forest.
The leaves on the maple trees were
fresh
and green,
and the creatures — the
four-footers and the
wings
of the air —
were all dancing,
dancing the mating dance.
The wind was quick
and fresh,
the stream was swift
and pure,
and the songs they made
as they danced through
the leaves
and over the
rocks

were songs of
beginning.
This song is a happy song that
each of us may
learn
and then sing once or twice before
it is time to teach it to
our children.
   My strong sons,
my beautiful daughters,
this old man who sits before you
has sung the song of
beginning life.
He has danced with Tashina the
mating dance,
and children and children's children
have walked
the earth.
And now in his winter
the sun
has warmed him once more, and
the Great Wanken tanka has allowed him
to dance again
with happiness,
as he has watched his sons become
men,
as he has watched his daughters become
women.
   But now the sun has fallen into
the earth,
and his last dance
is finished.
It is now his turn
to nourish the
earth
while his spirit
walks on the
wind

into the land of
the west,
where those who have gone
before
await him.
This he does that your own songs may be
sung.
This he does that your own dances may be
danced.
    Little warriors,
Little mother,
Dancing Moon,
Little Feather,
take hold and cling to only good things,
for good things will always
bring happiness.
Cling to the earth,
for she is our mother.
Cling to what you know
is true,
even if you are like the tree
in the meadow,
all alone.
Cling to compassion,
even when the one you care for
has been,
or will yet be,
your enemy.
Cling to what you must do,
no matter how difficult
the task
becomes.
Cling to life,
for in each new day
the Great Wanken tanka
has hidden a little happiness.
We have but to find it, and then
it is ours forever.
Finally, cling to this wrinkled old hand

even when it has gone away
from you.
Cling tightly to all of these things,
and you will be
the men
you wish to be,
the women
you wish to be.

Happy Wind gently squeezed the old man's neck while a tear from her eyes rolled down his wrinkled cheek. Slowly then the boys walked past him, holding his hand for a moment in manly dignity before they retired. At last Dancing Moon and Little Feather, with tears in their eyes, walked up to the old man. Carefully he took their hands and gently he squeezed them, telling them better in that way than he could in any other that he loved them and was pleased with their happiness. Then he pulled the robe over himself and hoped he would be able to sleep a little.

Through the night his pain was worse even than it had been the night before, and so, long after the others slept, he tossed and turned about.

A bloodcurdling yell from outside the cave brought all inside to their feet. The old man, shocked that he had slept so soundly, took up his ax and, with a last look at his family, shuffled out of the sacred cave, beginning what he knew would be his final journey.

Up close the Crow, whose horse was wheeling and prancing about, was even more hideous than the old man remembered. Of course he knew that the years did that to a man, but on this Crow it was more than the years and the scar and the paint. It had much to do with the things the man had allowed himself to live with that were inside, in his heart.

For a moment, while the Crow stared in amazement at such an elder opponent, the old man wondered if he should have told his family, or if he should tell the Crow.

This is a strange thing, O Giver-of-life, he thought silently as he stood waiting, watching.

For more seasons than this old man
can remember
he has looked forward
to meeting this hated Crow
in battle,
this Crow who took from him his
wife,
his son.
Now that such a moment
is here,
this man can find in his heart
no anger, no bitterness, no
desire
to kill.
For this despised Crow
whose emptiness of
life
shows darkly from
his face,
this aging warrior feels
only sorrow, only
pity.

The Crow, angry at the humiliation of fighting a man even older than himself, shouted with disgust as he reigned his horse back, waiting. The old man, knowing what must come, shook his stone ax in the air and tottered forward, taunting the Crow into battle. He was vaguely aware of his family in the background, though he did not dare turn his head to look at them. Yet all of them, including the staggering Smiling Wolf, had come from the cave and were intently watching.

Still the Crow hesitated, and so the old man threatened again with his ax, wondering at the strange expression on his opponent's face. But then he heard faintly the sound of hooves, and he stepped aside just in time to avoid the rush of his son's white war-horse, the war-horse upon which was seated . . . the captive Crow?

With shock showing on the old man's face, he watched as the two Crow warriors confronted each other. There was a brief

exchange of words, an angry snarl, and then with a crash the
two came together. Both reeled under the impact of the other's
blows, turned their mounts, and came at each other again, the
confrontation knocking both riders into the snow. Hastily they
were on their feet, circling each other warily. He of the disfigured eye feinted, then sprang in quickly, catching the other
off balance. Swinging his ax he hit the captive Crow, the one
with the red headdress, a glancing blow to the shoulder. Losing
his ax, the heavy blow sent the captive Crow reeling. Following
up too quickly the Crow with the disfigured eye found his
wounded opponent ducking under his punishing blow to pound
him in the stomach and throat with his fist. Surprised and in
great pain, he of the disfigured eye backed up to catch his
breath, wondering at this warrior whom he had despised as a
woman for so long.

Cautiously they circled again, the one brandishing his ax
menacingly, the other holding a small stone knife out before
him. Suddenly they were together again, and then the captive
Crow was being driven back, back, relentlessly back by his
older opponent. Twice he almost went down under the vicious
blows he was receiving, but then he backed into the stump of an
ancient pine, and from there he could go no further.

With a wicked snarl he of the disfigured eye lifted his ax into
the air and brought it down swiftly, the hatred in his heart
showing vividly on his face. Desperately, at the last instant, the
captive Crow twisted his head to one side and as his opponent's
ax buried itself in the wood he swung upward with his open
hand, catching the man's chin in his palm and snapping his head
backward. Instantly he of the red headdress followed up his
advantage, swinging with another blow and then a kick that
sent the Crow of the disfigured eye reeling into the snow, where
he lay unarmed.

Quickly the younger man was astride his chest, his knife at
the Crow's throat. With a savage snarl he ripped at the leather
shirt, tearing it open, exposing the throbbing pulse in the man's
neck.

This man is Cheyenne, he hissed in the man's ear, *not Crow!*

Then with a quick slice he cut a leather thong which hung
around the neck of his opponent, pulling it loose. Cautiously

then the captive Crow rose to his feet, freeing the man beneath
him. Then, with his hand, he made the sign that he of the disfigured eye was free to go, so long as he did so in peace.

For a long moment the Crow on the ground stared at him, not
yet fully understanding. But then he nodded, remembering the
time many seasons before when he had taken the amulet from
the young captive brave. Slowly he rose to his feet.

With dignity he of the red headdress turned his back on the
older Crow and walked slowly back toward where the family
waited in silence. Standing at last before them he gazed into the
eyes of each, turning last to the old man, to whom he held out
his hand. The old man gasped in amazement, for there, dan-
gling before him, was an amulet, identical to the ones worn by
himself and his son, Smiling Wolf.

This man is Cheyenne, the young warrior said softly and with
great emotion. *His name is Grey Hawk, and by right he is of
this lodge, this family. Do they accept him?*

Then he bared his shoulder and showed them the old wounds
the giant bear had given him as a tiny boy, the old wounds that
were now just fading scars. Then again he repeated his question.

Do the people of this lodge accept this warrior?

For a moment no one moved, and then the old man reached
out and tenderly took hold of the shoulder of him who had been
lost for so many seasons. Smiling Wolf, supported by his wives,
stepped forward and did the same. The three held to each other
in silence, and then all turned as they heard a sound behind
them.

He of the disfigured eye, mounted on his horse, was staring
now in disbelief, in shocked understanding. At last he recognized, at last he knew who the old man was, and as he understood, a measure of peace crept quietly into his heart. Without a
word then he turned and rode into the trees, knowing that a
portion of his life had closed forever.

That day was one of happiness for the old man, and despite
the pain in his wrinkled body, his soul was at peace with all
around him. Much later, long after all were asleep, he struggled
quietly to his feet, wrapped the bearskin about himself, took

one long look at those he loved so dearly, and shuffled out of
the lodge.

At once his horse was there, the buffalo runner that had come
to him so mysteriously. Together they walked to a low
hummock, and from that the old man was able to climb to the
horse's back. Quietly then he rode out of the clearing, not seeing
at all the tear-stained faces that watched his leaving. Up through
the aspen he rode, the aspen with their white spectral trunks
glowing softly in the darkness. And then he rode through the
soft blackness of the fragrant pine and fir, always upward,
always higher.

At last he emerged from the canyon, and on the top of a high
hill the horse paused, giving the old man a chance to feel the
night.

Grandfather,
this old creation of yours
loves the darkness.
Even the darkness
of old age
is beautiful.
The air is cold and clear,
and a moment ago, or
so it seems,
he smelled the woodsmoke from where
his family sleeps
around the fire.
How is it that
with all else almost gone,
he is still able to smell?
For little things like that this tired old man
gives thanks.
Now he is here,
alone.
Once he would have worried
that thought,
like a dog worrying a bone,
till it left him filled

with sadness.
But now, Grandfather,
such thoughts no longer affect him.
He is unmoved.
Everything has passed beyond him
and there are no new losses left
to fear.
No, not even death.
So many things that once seemed
important
no longer have significance.
Acquiring horses,
seeking fame,
knowing victory—
somehow it is too late
to worry about
all that.
Somehow it is too late
to . . .
Ah, Grandfather,
what a fine joke
this has been,
saving such a good portion of
this man's life
until he thought his life
was past.
Thank you for allowing him to be
a teacher,
to be a part of his
family
once more.
Thank you for allowing him to meet his brother
the bear
once more.
And, Hoka-hey,
wasn't that a fine battle
the little ones
fought?
Grandfather, did you see the way

our children put
those Crows to
rout?
And Dancing Moon and Little Feather,
did you see how . . .

And the old man broke into a happy chuckle, thinking about his family.

Most of all, Grandfather,
thank you for allowing this old man,
this old fool,
to see his son, his
lost son, once more,
and to have both sons,
at last,
together.
Thank you for allowing him
to see
with the eyes of his feelings
the life,
the love,
the happiness
in their eyes.
That is a memory he
will cherish
always.
But now what,
O Great One?
This man aches with longing for Tashina.
Still, he will do as you . . .

At that moment a strong warm wind drifted up out of the canyon, a wind that caught at the bearskin and at the white hair that Dancing Moon had so carefully braided for the old man. The horse stirred, and the warrior felt stabs of pain as his old bones groaned anew, pain that he was certain would never end.

But then quickly it did, and he wondered at the ease with which he turned upon the horse's back to see the dawn. For it was dawn, suddenly, and now he wondered how it had grown light so quickly, without his noticing that it was coming.

The dawn! The old man could see the —

Again the wind gusted out of the canyon, and as it did so the old man heard his name, from far off in the west someone was calling his name. Straining his eyes against the glare, he struggled to see who it was who knew his youth name and who called him. And then he did see, coming down the side of a beautiful hill, and his heart leaped within him.

Tashina!

Tashina, the bride of his youth, the life of his heart. She who had waited, she who had . . .

And then suddenly the old man knew that he had but to step out. Hesitantly he did so, first one step and then another. Then, with excitement mounting, he ran three or four steps. And he did it easily, without pain. Suddenly he threw back his head and laughed, laughed with joy and happiness so pure that it amazed even himself.

Suddenly Tashina stood before him, somehow changed and yet still beautiful, more beautiful even than he remembered her.

Hesitantly he moved toward her, fearing that she would vanish as she had done so many times before. But she didn't and then they were together and were holding each other and she was real and they were laughing and they were walking off together, and he was no longer old, and the wind was blowing gently behind them, behind them and around them and beneath them, carrying them westward, westward toward the green, green hills.

And only a little distance away the horse nickered once and then moved off the hill, its empty burden already slipping from its back to return to Mother Earth. The old man was, at last, the Windwalker.